THE HOUNDS OF HELL

THE HOUNDS
OF HELL

Stories of Canine Horror and Fantasy

Edited by

MICHEL PARRY

TAPLINGER PUBLISHING CO., INC.
NEW YORK

First published in the United States in 1974 by
TAPLINGER PUBLISHING CO., INC.
New York, New York

Library of Congress Catalog Card Number: 73-16635

ISBN 0-8008-3945-5

SECOND PRINTING

ACKNOWLEDGEMENTS

"The Hound" by H. P. Lovecraft © 1924 by the Rural Publishing Corporation. Reprinted by arrangement with the Scott Meredith Literary Agency.

"The Hound of Death" by Agatha Christie © 1924, 1926, 1929, 1934, 1971 by the Christie Copyright Trust. Reprinted from *The Golden Ball and Other Stories* by permission of the publishers, Dodd, Mead and Co. Inc., New York.

"Dead Dog" by Manly Wade Wellman © Street and Smith Publications Inc. for *Weird Tales*, August 1938. Reprinted by permission of the author.

"The Howling Tower" by Fritz Leiber © 1941 by Street & Smith Publications Inc. Reprinted by permission of the author and his agent, Leslie Flood.

"The White Dog" by Feodor Sologub, translated by John Cournos, reprinted from *The Old House and Other Stories* by permission of the publishers, Martin Secker Ltd.

"The Hound" by William Faulkner © 1931 and renewed 1959 by William Faulkner. Reprinted from *Dr. Martino and Other Stories* by permission of Random House, Inc., New York.

"The Hound of Pedro" by Robert Bloch © 1938 by Street & Smith Publications Inc. for *Weird Tales*, November 1938. Reprinted by arrangement with the Scott Meredith Literary Agency.

CONTENTS

As John Kembal was coming out of the Woods, there arose a little Black Cloud in the north-west and Kembal immediately felt a force upon him, which made him not able to avoid running upon the stumps of Trees, that were before him; albeit he had a broad plain cart-way before him; but tho' he had his Ax also on his Shoulder to endanger him in his Falls, he could not forebear going out of his way to tumble over them. When he came below the Meeting House, there appeared unto him, a little thing like a Puppy, of a Darkish Colour and it shot backwards and forwards between his legs. He had the courage to use all possible Endeavours of Cutting it with his Ax; but he could not hit it. The Puppy gave a jump from him, and went, as to him it seem'd into the Ground. Going a little further, there appeared unto him a Black Puppy, somewhat bigger than the first, but as black as a cole. Its Motions were quicker than those of his Ax; it flew at his Belly and away; then at his throat; so, over his shoulder one way, and then over his shoulder another way. His Heart now began to fail him, and he thought the Dog would have tore his throat out. But he recovered himself and called upon God in his distress; and naming the Name of JESUS CHRIST it vanished away at once.

COTTON MATHER
The Wonders of the Invisible World

INTRODUCTION

From yawning rifts, with many a yell,
Mix'd with sulphureous flames, ascend
The misbegotten dogs of Hell.
—Sir Walter Scott
The Wild Huntsman

"THE MOON *was shining bright upon the clearing, and there
in the centre lay the unhappy maid where she had fallen, dead
of fear and of fatigue. But it was not the sight of her body,
nor yet was it that of the body of Hugo Baskerville lying near
her, which raised the hair upon the heads of these three dare-
devil roysterers, but it was that, standing over Hugo, and
plucking at his throat, there stood a foul thing, a great, black
beast, shaped like a hound, yet larger than any hound that
ever mortal eye has rested upon. And even as they looked the
thing tore the throat out of Hugo Baskerville, on which, as it
turned its blazing eyes and dripping jaws upon them, the three
shrieked with fear and rode for dear life, still screaming, across
the moor."*

Few who have read this passage from Sir Arthur Conan
Doyle's *The Hound of the Baskervilles* can have escaped a
shuddery inner reaction. It seems to strike a primordial chord
of response deep within our racial memory, reminding us how
vulnerable we naked apes really are without our sophisticated
weaponry.

The lonely moor, the hapless human and, close on his heels,
the huge hound, black as sin with eyes like hot coals and jaws
slaveringly eager to close on a pulsing throat . . . all that's needed
to perfect the scene is the mournful blood-freezing howl across
the moor which inevitably precedes the fatal appearance of the
hound. The perennial fascination of such a confrontation between

hound and human is reflected in the popularity of Conan Doyle's novel, a world best-seller for over fifty years, and in the success of the many films it has inspired. It is also reflected in the sixteen stories brought together in this collection, stories of diverse dogs with but one thing in common: their bite is very much worse than their bark!

In *Beware of the Cat*, the companion volume to the present anthology, I offered the reader stories of feline fantasy and horror. The cat walks alone, mysterious, a creature of the night. It is not difficult to see why, for centuries, writers and artists have attributed it with malefic supernatural qualities. But of all creatures, the dog is supposed to be man's best friend. Why then the taste for stories in which we are hounded and torn by monster dogs? Partly, I think, because they touch upon the fear of man the hunter that he may himself one day be the hunted. And the irony is all the greater if it is his loyal four-legged friend that does the hunting.

No amount of mischief from the wayward cat is likely to surprise us. We almost expect it. But when the trusted dog turns suddenly upon us, baring his fangs, then are we truly shocked. There is something almost blasphemous in the image of that great black hound tearing at Hugo Baskerville's throat, man's best friend becoming man's worst *fiend*. It smacks, some-how, of cannibalism.*

Hell-hounds such as the one described by Conan Doyle abound in British folklore, particularly in the counties of Devon and Cornwall. The bleak expanse of Dartmoor, the setting of *The Hound of the Baskervilles*, is undoubtedly the most Hound-haunted area of the British Isles. Spectral dogs known as "Wish Hounds" or "Gabriel Hounds" have been seen and heard for centuries around the aptly-named Hound Tor and Hunt's Tor on Dartmoor. They are said to be the spirits of unbaptized children, doomed forever to angrily chase the Devil for obstructing their entry to Heaven. Nearby, at Hergest, there is a ghostly Black Hound and another to be found at Clyre Court,

---

* Certain Mongol tribes fed the bodies of their dead to packs of dogs living on an exclusive diet of human flesh.

the latter reputedly the one which inspired Conan Doyle to write his immortal novel. And not so far away in Cornwall lies Dogmere Moor across which the ghost of Evil Tregeagle, a local ne'er-do-well, is nightly chased by Satan and his pack of Hell-hounds. This story is closely related to the legend, popular throughout Northern Europe, of the Wild Huntsman and his pack of phantom hounds. Sometimes the hounds are headless, as is often the case with their Master; in other versions they have human heads. A French variation of the legend is the story of the evil knight Hellenquin and his Barons, condemned to hunt until domesday with their pack of demon-dogs.

Carmarthenshire and other parts of Wales are bedevilled by the banshee-like "Cwn Anwn" (Dogs of Hell) or Dogs of the Abyss. Their eerie baying is often to be heard during funerals as they impatiently wait to pursue the damned soul of a newly-buried miscreant. Like the hounds in Fritz Leiber's story, *The Howling Tower*, they are invisible. A particularly unpleasant Hell-hound is the "Mauthe Doog" which haunted the ancient castle of Peele in the Isle of Man. One venturesome soldier who tried to get a close look at it returned "stricken dumb with horror" to die after three days of unbearable agony.

No less daunting is the celebrated "Black Dogge of Newgate" described in a pamphlet written in 1538 by a rogue named Luke Hutton. Hutton relates how a famine during the reign of Henry III (1207–72) reduced the inmates of Newgate Prison to such a state of starvation that they were driven to eat each other. One of the first to be consumed was a scholar imprisoned for being a practitioner of "devilish witchcraft". Hutton tells us he provided "passing good meat". Afterwards, the scholar's ghost haunted his devourers to the death and subsequently took on the shape of a gigantic hound—"Black he was, with curling snakes for hair, his eyes like torches, his breath was poison and smoke came from his nostrils." Henceforth, Newgate was plagued by the Black Dog, the apparition usually appearing to condemned men on their last journey to the gallows.

"I will not request you, according to the old proverb to love me, love my hound," wrote Hutton, "but only love me, and

hang my Dogge, for he is not worthy so good a name as Hound."
Luke Hutton wrote his pamphlet as an exhortation to fellow
wrong-doers to mend their ways and so avoid becoming
acquainted with the Black Dog. Ironically, he fell back into his
former villainy and it is said his life ended on the gallows—at
Newgate Prison! No doubt the Black Dogge wagged its tail
with pleasure at the sight of him.

The dog's proverbial loyalty to man is an essential element
of many legends and of several of the stories in this book, such
loyalty often extending beyond death. It may be remembered
that Anubis, the dog-headed god of the Egyptians, was known
as the "Guardian of the Dead", as was Cerberus, the monstrous
three-headed watch-dog of Hades. Readers may find even the
latter preferable to the terrible guardian of the tomb described
in H. P. Lovecraft's *The Hound.* Lovecraft's story is reminiscent
of the legend of the Brixham Black Dog which haunts a house
to safeguard a treasure secreted there by its long-dead master
centuries before. For some reason, European Hell-hounds tend
to be black in colour whilst in Russia white dogs were until
recently viewed with especial dread—a fear effectively portrayed
in *The White Dog* by Feodor Sologub.

The theme of the dog so loyal that it avenges a murdered
master is a very ancient one. Modern variations on the theme
include *Dog or Demon?* by Theo Gift, *Staley Fleming's
Hallucination* by Ambrose Bierce and William Faulkner's *The
Hound.* The last story is set in the American South of recent
years, yet is remarkably similar to a French legend over six
hundred years old. In this, the dog's master, Aubry de
Montdidier, was murdered by his friend Macaire and his body
hidden in a wood. Eventually the faithful dog's efforts led to
the discovery of the body. The dog's hostility to Macaire
brought him under suspicion, and Charles VI ordered an ordeal
by combat, pitting Macaire against the dog. The dog won.

"Deliver my darling from the power of the Dog" beseeches
the Biblical Psalm and, certainly, throughout history dogs have
been somewhat unluckily credited with a variety of supernatural
powers which have led to their being ritually killed and/or eaten

in vast numbers. Even today certain American Indians and eastern cultures continue to eat dogs in order to gain strength and potency. In the Middle Ages, necromancers frequently employed a dog to search out the mandrake roots necessary for their sorceries.

Dogs also gained notoriety as witches' familiars, a dog-familiar bestowing a higher status upon the owner than a cat-familiar. Records of the witch trials have immortalized the names of some of these supposed dog-demons—"Elimanzar", "Grizzle", "Greedigut", "Vinegar Tom", and "Jamara", the last "like a fat spaniel without any legs at all". Then there were the were-dogs, humans who assumed the shape of dogs through the practice of Black Magic. Representative were-dogs in this collection are *The Hound of Pedro* by Robert Bloch and *The White Dog* by Feodor Sologub.

It was also once widely believed that the Devil's favourite guise for appearing to his followers was in the form of a dog, usually black. The literature of witchcraft is full of such claims. For instance, in 1556 one Mother Waterhouse confessed that Satan sported with her "in the lykeness of a great dogge". Margaret Barclay, executed for witchcraft in Ayrshire in 1613, allegedly received the visit of the Devil in the shape of a handsome brown lap-dog "which emmited flashes from its jaws and nostrils to illuminate the witches during the performance of the spell". Dogs and Devils, it would seem, are inextricably bound up with one another.

Finally, a word of warning. This book is not recommended for reading aloud to one's dog as some people are in the habit of doing. Nor should it be allowed to fall into the wrong paws. If it does, you may find that your dog has a bone to pick with you. Take care. The bone may be one of your own.

And now to let slip the dogs of Fear . . .

MICHEL PARRY

THE HOUND

by H. P. Lovecraft

DURING HIS OWN *life-time, the work of the great American fantasy writer Howard Phillips Lovecraft (1890–1937) was relegated to the pulp magazines. Only after his death did his stories achieve the hardback publication they rightly deserved, thanks largely to the efforts of a band of Lovecraft devotees led by August Derleth. Lovecraft's literary reputation is now firmly if grudgingly established and forty years after his death his work is more popular than ever he could have imagined, young people, in particular, finding a new post-psychedelic relevance to Lovecraft's intimations of cosmic depths. In the last few years sales of his books have reached well over a million in the United States alone.*

As I noted in my previous anthology, Beware of the Cat, *Lovecraft held the canine species in disdain, preferring the company of the "cool, lithe, cynical" cat. Undoubtedly his antipathy to dogs helped Lovecraft conceive of the monstrous hybrid depicted in* The Hound, *one of his most nightmarish tales and one in which the influence of Poe is much in evidence.*

In my tortured ears there sounds unceasingly a nightmare whirring and flapping, and a faint, distant baying as of some gigantic hound. It is not dream—it is not, I fear, even madness —for too much has already happened to give me these merciful doubts.

St John is a mangled corpse; I alone know why, and such is my knowledge that I am about to blow out my brains for fear I shall be mangled in the same way. Down unlit and illimitable corridors of eldritch phantasy sweeps the black, shapeless Nemesis that drives me to self-annihilation.

May heaven forgive the folly and morbidity which led us both to so monstrous a fate! Wearied with the commonplaces of a prosaic world; where even the joys of romance and adventure soon grow stale. St John and I had followed enthusiastically every aesthetic and intellectual movement which promised respite from our devastating ennui. The enigmas of the symbolists and the ecstasies of the pre-Raphaelites all were ours in their time, but each new moon was drained too soon, of its diverting novelty and appeal.

Only the sombre philosophy of the decadents could help us, and this we found potent only by increasing gradually the depth and diabolism of our penetrations. Baudelaire and Huysmans were soon exhausted of thrills, till finally there remained for us only the more direct stimuli of unnatural personal experiences and adventures. It was this frightful emotional need which led us eventually to that detestable course which even in my present fear I mention with shame and timidity—that hideous extremity of human outrage, and abhorred practice of grave-robbing.

I cannot reveal the details of our shocking expeditions, or catalogue even partly the worst of the trophies adorning the nameless museum we prepared in the great stone house where we jointly dwelt, alone and servantless. Our museum was a blasphemous, unthinkable place, where with the satanic taste of neurotic virtuosi we had assembled a universe of terror and decay to excite our jaded sensibilities. It was a secret room, far, far, underground; where huge winged daemons carven of basalt and onyx vomited from wide grinning mouths weird green and orange light, and hidden pneumatic pipes ruffled into kaleidoscopic dances of death the lines of red charnel things hand in hand woven in voluminous black hangings. Through these pipes came at will the odours our moods most craved; sometimes the scent of pale funeral lilies, sometimes the narcotic incense of imagined Eastern shrines of the kingly dead, and sometimes—

how I shudder to recall it!—the frightful, soul-upheaving stenches of the uncovered grave.

Around the walls of this repellent chamber were cases of antique mummies alternating with comely, lifelike bodies perfectly stuffed and cured by the taxidermist's art, and with headstones snatched from the oldest churchyards of the world. Niches here and there contained skulls of all shapes, and heads preserved in various stages of dissolution. There one might find the rotting, bald pates of famous noblemen, and the fresh and radiantly golden heads of new-buried children.

Statues and paintings there were, all of fiendish subjects and some executed by St John and myself. A locked portfolio, bound in tanned human skin, held certain unknown and unnamable drawings which it was rumoured Goya had perpetrated but dared not acknowledge. There were nauseous musical instruments, stringed, brass, and wood-wind, on which St John and I sometimes produced dissonances of exquisite morbidity and cacodaemoniacal ghastliness; whilst in a multitude of inlaid ebony cabinets reposed the most incredible and unimaginable variety of tomb-loot ever assembled by human madness and perversity. It is of this loot in particular that I must not speak—thank God I had the courage to destroy it long before I thought of destroying myself!

The predatory excursions on which we collected our unmentionable treasures were always artistically memorable events. We were no vulgar ghouls, but worked only under certain conditions of mood, landscape, environment, weather, season, and moonlight. These pastimes were to us the most exquisite form of aesthetic expression, and we gave their details a fastidious technical care. An inappropriate hour, a jarring lighting effect, or a clumsy manipulation of the damp sod, would almost totally destroy for us that ecstatic titillation which followed the exhumation of some ominous, grinning secret of the earth. Our quest for novel scenes and piquant conditions was feverish and insatiate—St John was always the leader, and he it was who led the way at last to that mocking, accursed spot which brought us our hideous and inevitable doom.

By what malign fatality were we lured to that terrible Holland churchyard? I think it was the dark rumour and legendry, the tales of one buried for five centuries, who had himself been a ghoul in his time and had stolen a potent thing from a mighty sepulchre. I can recall the scene in these final moments—the pale autumnal moon over the graves, casting long horrible shadows; the grotesque trees, drooping sullenly to meet the neglected grass and the crumbling slabs; the vast legions of strangely colossal bats that flew against the moon; the antique ivied church pointing a huge spectral finger at the livid sky, the phosphorescent insects that danced like death-fires under the yews in a distant corner; the odours of mould, vegetation, and less explicable things that mingled feebly with the night-wind from over far swamps and seas; and, worst of all, the faint deep-toned baying of some gigantic hound which we could neither see nor definitely place. As we heard this suggestion of baying we shuddered, remembering the tales of the peasantry; for he whom we sought had centuries before been found in this self-same spot, torn and mangled by the claws and teeth of some unspeakable beast.

I remember how we delved in the ghoul's grave with our spades, and how we thrilled at the picture of ourselves, the grave, the pale watching moon, the horrible shadows, the grotesque trees, the titanic bats, the antique church, the dancing death-fires, the sickening odours, the gentle moaning night-wind, and the strange, half-heard directionless baying of whose objective existence we could scarcely be sure.

Then we struck a substance harder than the damp mould, and beheld a rotting oblong box crusted with mineral deposits from the long undisturbed ground. It was incredibly tough and thick, but so old that we finally prized it open and feasted our eyes on what it held.

Much—amazingly much—was left of the object despite the lapse of five hundred years. The skeleton, though crushed in places by the jaws of the thing that had killed it, held together with surprising firmness, and we gloated over the clean white skull and its long, firm teeth and its eyeless sockets that once had glowed with a charnel fever like our own. In the coffin lay an amulet of curious and exotic design, which had apparently been worn around the sleeper's neck. It was the oddly conventionalized figure of a crouching winged hound, or sphinx with a semi-canine face, and was exquisitely carved in antique Oriental fashion from a small piece of green jade. The expression of its features was repellent in the extreme, savouring at once of death, bestiality, and malevolence. Around the base was an inscription in characters which neither St John nor I could identify; and on the bottom, like a maker's seal, was given a grotesque and formidable skull.

Immediately upon beholding this amulet we knew that we must possess it; that this treasure alone was our logical pelt from the centuried grave. Even had its outlines been unfamiliar we would have desired it, but as we looked more closely we saw that it was not wholly unfamiliar. Alien it indeed was to all art and literature which sane and balanced readers know, but we recognized it as the thing hinted of in the forbidden *Necronomicon* at the mad Arab Abdul Alhazred; the ghastly soul-symbol of the corpse-eating cult of inaccessible Leng, in Central Asia. All too well did we trace the sinister lineaments described by the old Arab deamonologist; lineaments, he wrote, drawn from some obscure supernatural manifestation of the souls of those who vexed and gnawed at the dead.

Seizing the green jade object, we gave a last glance at the bleached and cavern-eyed face of its owner and closed up the grave as we found it. As we hastened from the abhorrent spot, the stolen amulet in St John's pocket, we thought we saw the bats descend in a body to the earth we had so lately rifled, as if seeking for some cursed and unholy nourishment. But the autumn moon shone weak and pale, and we could not be sure.

So, too, as we sailed the next day away from Holland to our home, we thought we heard the faint distant baying of some gigantic hound in the background. But the autumn wind moaned sad and wan, and we could not be sure.

Less than a week after our return to England, strange things began to happen. We lived as recluses; devoid of friends, alone, and without servants in a few rooms of an ancient manor-house on a bleak and unfrequented moor; so that our doors were seldom disturbed by the knock of the visitor.

Now, however, we were troubled by what seemed to be a frequent fumbling in the night, not only around the doors but around the windows also, upper as well as lower. Once we fancied that a large, opaque body darkened the library window when the moon was shining against it, and another time we thought we heard a whirring or flapping sound not far off. On each occasion investigation revealed nothing, and we began to ascribe the occurrences to imagination which still prolonged in our ears the faint far baying we thought we had heard in the Holland churchyard. The jade amulet now reposed in a niche in our museum, and sometimes we burned a strangely scented candle before it. We read much in Alhazred's *Necronomicon* about its properties, and about the relation of ghosts' souls to the objects it symbolized; and were disturbed by what we read.

Then terror came.

On the night of September 24th, 19—, I heard a knock at my chamber door. Fancying it St John's, I bade the knocker enter, but was answered only by a shrill laugh. There was no one in the corridor. When I aroused St John from his sleep, he professed entire ignorance of the event, and became as worried as I. It was the night that the faint, distant baying over the moor became to us a certain and dreaded reality.

Four days later, whilst we were both in the hidden museum, there came a low, cautious scratching at the single door which led to the secret library staircase. Our alarm was now divided, for, besides our fear of the unknown, we had always entertained a dread that our grisly collection might be discovered. Extinguishing all lights, we proceeded to the door and threw it suddenly open; whereupon we felt an unaccountable rush of air, and heard, as if receding far away, a queer combination of rustling, tittering, and articulate chatter. Whether we were mad, dreaming, or in our senses, we did not try to determine. We only realized, with the blackest of apprehensions, that the apparently disembodied chatter was beyond a doubt *in the Dutch language.*

After that we lived in growing horror and fascination. Mostly we held to the theory that we were jointly going mad from our life of unnatural excitements, but sometimes it pleased us more to dramatize ourselves as the victims of some creeping and appalling doom. Bizarre manifestations were now too frequent to count. Our lonely house was seemingly alive with the presence of some malign being whose nature we could not guess, and every night that daemoniac baying rolled over the wind-swept moor, always louder and louder. On October 29 we found in the soft earth underneath the library window a series of footprints utterly impossible to describe. They were as baffling as the hordes of great bats which haunted the old manor-house in unprecedented and increasing numbers.

The horror reached a culmination on November 18, when St John, walking home after dark from the dismal railway station, was seized by some frightful carnivorous thing and torn to ribbons. His screams had reached the house, and I had hastened to the terrible scene in time to hear a whir of wings and see a vague black cloudy thing silhouetted against the rising moon.

My friend was dying when I spoke to him, and he could not answer coherently. All he could do was to whisper, "The amulet —that damned thing—"

Then he collapsed, an inert mass of mangled flesh.

I buried him the next midnight in one of our neglected gardens, and mumbled over his body one of the devilish rituals he had loved in life. And as I pronounced the last daemoniac sentence I heard afar on the moor the faint baying of some gigantic hound. The moon was up, but I dared not look at it. And when I saw on the dim-lighted moor a wide nebulous shadow sweeping from mound to mound, I shut my eyes and threw myself face down upon the ground. When I arose, trembling, I know not how much later, I staggered into the house and made shocking obeisances before the enshrined amulet of green jade.

Being now afraid to live alone in the ancient house on the

moor, I departed on the following day for London, taking with
me the amulet after destroying by fire and burial the rest of the
impious collection in the museum. But after three nights I heard
the baying again, and before a week was over felt strange eyes
upon me whenever it was dark. One evening as I strolled on
Victoria Embankment for some needed air, I saw a black shape
obscure one of the reflections of the lamps in the water. A
wind, stronger than the night-wind, rushed by, and I knew
that what had befallen St John must soon befall me.

The next day I carefully wrapped the green jade amulet and
sailed for Holland. What mercy I might gain by returning the
thing to its silent, sleeping owner I knew not; but I felt that I
must try any step conceivably logical. What the hound was, and
why it had pursued me, were questions still vague; but I had
first heard the baying in that ancient churchyard, and every
subsequent event including St John's dying whisper had served
to connect the curse with the stealing of the amulet. Accordingly
I sank into the nethermost abysses of despair when, at an inn in
Rotterdam, I discovered that thieves had despoiled me of this
sole means of salvation.

The baying was loud that evening, and in the morning I read
of a nameless deed in the vilest quarter of the city. The rabble
were in terror, for upon an evil tenement had fallen a red death
beyond the foulest previous crime of the neighbourhood. In a
squalid thieves' den an entire family had been torn to shreds by
an unknown thing which left no trace, and those around had
heard all night a faint, deep, insistent note as of a gigantic
hound.

So at last I stood again in the unwholesome churchyard where
a pale winter moon cast hideous shadows, and leafless trees
drooped sullenly to meet the withered, frosty grass and cracking
slabs, and the ivied church pointed a jeering finger at the unfriendly sky, and the night-wind howled maniacally from over
frozen swamps and frigid seas. The baying was very faint now,
and it ceased altogether as I approached the ancient grave I had
once violated, and frightened away an abnormally large horde
of bats which had been hovering curiously around it.

I know not why I went thither unless to pray, or gibber out insane pleas and apologies to the calm white thing that lay within; but, whatever my reason, I attacked the half-frozen sod with a desperation partly mine and partly that of a dominating will outside myself. Excavation was much easier than I expected, though at one point I encountered a queer interruption; when a lean vulture darted down out of the cold sky and pecked frantically at the grave-earth until I killed him with a blow of my spade. Finally I reached the rotting oblong box and removed the damp nitrous cover. This is the last rational act I ever performed.

For crouched within that centuried coffin, embraced by a close-packed nightmare retinue of high, sinewy, sleeping bats, was the bony thing my friend and I had robbed; not clean and placid as we had seen it then, but covered with caked blood and shreds of alien flesh and hair, and leering sentiently at me with phosphorescent sockets and sharp ensanguined fangs yawning twistedly in mockery of my inevitable doom. And when it gave from those grinning jaws a deep, sardonic bay as of some gigantic hound, and I saw that it held in its gory filthy claw the lost and fateful amulet of green jade, I merely screamed and ran away idiotically, my screams soon dissolving into peals of hysterical laughter.

Madness rides the star-wind... claws and teeth sharpened on centuries of corpses... dripping death astride a bacchanale of bats from night-black ruins of buried temples of Belial... Now, as the baying of that dead fleshless monstrosity grows louder and louder, and the stealthy whirring and flapping of those accursed web-wings circles closer and closer, I shall seek with my revolver the oblivion which is my only refuge from the unnamed and unnamable.

STALEY FLEMING'S HALLUCINATION

by Ambrose Bierce

"THE DOG IS *a detestable quadruped that knows more ways to be unmentionable than can be named in seven languages." So wrote the American cynic and satirist Ambrose Bierce (1842–1914), who disappeared in mysterious circumstances during Pancho Villa's Mexican revolution and was never seen again. Bierce's dislike of dogs seems to have been obsessive: his poem "The Oakland Dog" offers a blissful idyllic vision of a world rid of all canines. And in a well-known essay he made the Swiftian suggestion of supplying hungry prospectors in the distant Klondike with cans of dog-meat: "it is honestly rank and strong and has plenty of 'chew' in it—just the right kind of meat for founders of empires and heralds of civilization . . ."*

Of two men who were talking one was a physician.

"I sent for you, Doctor," said the other, "but I don't think you can do me any good. Maybe you can recommend a specialist in psychopathy. I fancy I'm a bit loony."

"You look all right," the physician said.

"You shall judge—I have hallucinations. I wake every night and see in my room, intently watching me, a big black Newfoundland dog with a white forefoot."

"You say you wake; are you sure about that? 'Hallucinations' are sometimes only dreams."

"Oh, I wake all right. Sometimes I lie still a long time, looking at the dog as earnestly as the dog looks at me—I always leave the light going. When I can't endure it any longer I sit up in bed—and nothing is there!"

"'M, 'm—what is the beast's expression?'"

"It seems to me sinister. Of course I know that, except in art, an animal's face in repose has always the same expression. But this is not a real animal. Newfoundland dogs are pretty mild-looking, you know; what's the matter with this one?"

"Really, my diagnosis would have no value: I am not going to treat the dog."

The physician laughed at his own pleasantry, but narrowly watched his patient from the corner of his eye. Presently he said: "Fleming, your description of the beast fits the dog of the late Atwell Barton."

Fleming half rose from his chair, sat again and made a visible attempt at indifference. "I remember Barton," he said; "I believe he was—it was reported that—wasn't there something suspicious in his death?"

Looking squarely now into the eyes of his patient, the physician said: "Three years ago the body of your old enemy, Atwell Barton, was found in the woods near his house and yours. He had been stabbed to death. There have been no arrests; there was no clue. Some of us had 'theories'. I had one. Have you?"

"I? Why, bless your soul, what could I know about it? You remember that I left for Europe almost immediately afterwards —a considerable time afterwards. In the few weeks since my return you could not expect me to construct a 'theory'. In fact, I have not given the matter a thought. What about his dog?"

"It was first to find the body. It died of starvation on his grave."

We do not know the inexorable law underlying coincidences. Staley Fleming did not, or he would perhaps not have sprung to his feet as the night wind brought in through the open window the long wailing howl of a distant dog. He strode several times across the room in the steadfast gaze of the physician; then, abruptly confronting him, almost shouted: "What has all this to do with my trouble, Dr Halderman? You forget why you were sent for."

Rising, the physician laid his hand upon his patient's arm and said, gently: "Pardon me. I cannot diagnose your disorder offhand—tomorrow, perhaps. Please go to bed, leaving your door unlocked; I will pass the night here with your books. Can you call me without rising?"

"Yes, there is an electric bell."

"Good. If anything disturbs you push the button without sitting up. Good night."

Comfortably installed in an arm-chair the man of medicine stared into the glowing coals and thought deeply and long, but apparently to little purpose, for he frequently rose and opening a door leading to the staircase, listened intently; then resumed his seat. Presently, however, he fell asleep, and when he woke it was past midnight. He stirred the failing fire, lifted a book from the table at his side and looked at the title. It was Denneker's *Meditations.* He opened it at random and began to read:

> "Forasmuch as it is ordained of God that all flesh hath spirit and thereby taketh on spiritual powers, so, also, the spirit hath powers of the flesh, even when it is gone out of the flesh and liveth as a thing apart, as many a violence performed by wraith and lemure sheweth. And there be who say that man is not single in this, but the beasts have the like evil inducement, and—"

The reading was interrupted by a shaking of the house, as by the fall of a heavy object. The reader flung down the book, rushed from the room and mounted the stairs to Fleming's bed-chamber. He tried the door, but contrary to his instructions it was locked. He set his shoulder against it with such force that it gave way. On the floor near the disordered bed, in his night-clothes, lay Fleming, gasping away his life.

The physician raised the dying man's head from the floor and observed a wound in the throat. "I should have thought of this," he said, believing it suicide.

When the man was dead an examination disclosed the unmistakable marks of an animal's fangs deeply sunken into the jugular vein.

But there was no animal.

THE DOG

by Ivan Turgenev

DESPITE BEING BORN *into a wealthy land-owning family, Ivan Sergevich Turgenev (1818–1883) was passionately anti-Establishment. One of Russia's most celebrated writers and dramatists, he employed his talent to expose the horrors of the feudal system persisting under the Tsar in the nineteenth century. Most of his writing is in the vein of social realism but as he grew older Turgenev became increasingly fascinated by the supernatural, a fascination vividly reflected in his tale of* The Dog . . .

"But if you once admit the existence of the supernatural, and that it can enter into the ordinary affairs of everyday life, allow me to ask what scope is left for the exercise of reason?"

And so saying, Anthony Stephanich crossed his arms.

Anthony Stephanich was a Councillor to the Minister in some department or other, and this circumstance, joined with those of his possessing a grave bass voice, and of his speaking with great precision, rendered him an object of universal consideration. He had just been compelled, as his detractors phrased it, to accept the Cross of St Stanislaus.

"There can be no doubt of that," said Skorevich.

"It is impossible to dispute it," said Cinarevich.

"I assent entirely," said the master of the house, Phinoplentoff, in his thin little voice.

Now there was a short, plump, bald, middle-aged little man who was sitting silent close to the stove, and he suddenly said—

"I confess that I don't agree with you, for something which was certainly supernatural once happened to me myself."

Everybody looked at him, and there was a pause. The little man in question was a small landed proprietor in Kalouga who had only come to live at St Petersburg a short time before. He had once been in the hussars and lost his money at play, resigned his commission, and returned to cultivate cabbages at his native village. Recent events had greatly reduced his income, and he had come to town in order to try and obtain some small employment. For this object he had none of the ordinary means of success, nor influential acquaintances, but he placed great confidence in the friendship of an old comrade in his regiment, who had certainly become a great personage, how or why nobody knew, and whom he had once helped to thrash a card-sharper. Besides this, he was a great believer in his own luck, and, as a matter of fact, his confidence turned out not to have been misplaced. After some days he was appointed inspector of certain government factories. The place was a good one, it stood rather high, and did not call for the exercise of any striking talents even if the factories in question had existed anywhere except upon paper, or if it had been settled what was to be manufactured in them when they did exist. But then they formed part of a new scheme of administrative economy.

Anthony Stephanich was the first to speak.

"Surely, my dear sir, you cannot mean seriously to tell us that you ever met with anything supernatural; I mean, any departure from the laws of nature."

"Yes, I did," said the "dear sir", whose name was Porphyry Capitonovich.

"A departure from the laws of nature," sharply repeated Anthony Stephanich, who had evidently got hold of a favourite phrase.

"Quite so; just as you are kind enough to express it," said the little man.

"This is very extraordinary. What do you think, gentlemen?"

Anthony Stephanich had tried to put on a sarcastic expression, but had failed; or, to be more exact, had given his features an expression such as would have been produced by perceiving a bad smell. He turned to the gentlemen from Kalouga and continued—

"Could you be so kind as to give us some details of such a strange occurrence?"

"Do you want to hear about it?" said the gentleman. "All right."

He got up, went to the middle of the room, and began.

"You may possibly know, gentlemen, or more probably you don't, that I possess a small property in the district of Kozelsk. I used to get something from it once upon a time, but, as you may well conceive, it brings me in nothing now, except business and quarrels. However, I don't want to talk politics. Well, on this property I had a small farm with a kitchen-garden to match, a pond with tench in it, divers buildings, and among others a little house for myself. I am not married. One fine day, six years ago, I came home rather late. I had been dining with one of the neighbours, but I assure you I was all right so far as that went. I took off my clothes, got into bed, and blew out the candle. I had hardly blown it out when I heard something move underneath the bed. I wondered what it could be. At first I thought it was mice. But it wasn't mice. I could hear it scratching and walking about and shaking itself. It was obvious that it was a dog, but I couldn't think what dog it could be. I hadn't got one. So I thought that it must be a stray one. I called the servant and scolded him for being careless, and letting a dog get hidden under the bed. He asked, "What dog?" I answered him, "How should I know?" It was his business to prevent that sort of thing happening. He stooped down with the candle and looked under the bed. He said there was not any dog there. I looked underneath myself, and sure enough there was no dog there. I stared at him, and he began to grin. I called him a fool, and said the dog must have slipped out and got away when he opened the door, that he had been half asleep and hadn't noticed it. I asked if he thought that I had been drinking? However, I did not await the reply which he was about to make, but told him to clear out. When he was gone, I curled myself up, and I heard nothing more that night.

"However, the night afterwards the whole thing began again. I had hardly put the candle out when I heard the beast shake itself. I called the servant again. He looked under the bed. There wasn't anything there. So I sent him away again, and put out the candle the second time. Then I heard the dog again. There couldn't be any doubt about it. I could hear it breathe. I could hear it biting at its own coat and hunting for fleas, so I called the man to come again, without bringing a candle. He came, and I told him to listen. He said he heard. I couldn't see him, but I knew by the sound of his voice that he was frightened. I asked him how he could explain it. He said it was the Evil One. I told him to hold his stupid tongue, but we were both pretty frightened. I lighted the candle, and then there was no more dog and no more noise. I left the candle burning all night, and whether you like to believe it or not, I assure you that the same thing went on every night for six weeks. I got quite used to it, and I used to put out the candle, because light prevents my sleeping, and I did not mind the thing, as it didn't do me any harm."

"You are certainly brave," said Anthony Stephanich, with a smile of mingled pity and contempt. "One can see that you have been a trooper."

"I certainly shouldn't be afraid of you, at any rate," answered Porphyry Capitonovich, with a decided ring of the soldier in his tone. "Anyhow, I'll tell you what happened. The same neighbour with whom I had dined before came to dine with me in turn. He took pot-luck with me, and I won fifteen roubles from him afterwards. He looked out into the night, and said he would have to be going. However, I had a plan, and I asked him to stay and sleep, and try and win his money back the next day. He considered, and then he agreed to stay. I had a bed made up for him in my own room. We went to bed and smoked and talked and discussed women, as men do. At last I saw that Basil Basilich put out his light and turned his back towards me, as much as to say *Schlafen Sie wohl.* I waited a little, and then I put out my own candle, and before I had time to think the game began. The beast did more than move; he came out from under the bed, and walked across the room. I could hear his feet on the wooden floor. He shook himself, and then there was a thump. He knocked against a chair, which was standing beside Basil Basilich's bed. Basil called out to me quite naturally, in his ordinary voice, to ask me if the dog that I had got was a pointer. I told him that I hadn't got any dog, and never had had. He asked me what the noise was then? I told him to light his candle and see. He asked me again if it wasn't a dog. Then I heard him turn round. He told me I was joking; and I told him I was not.

"After this I heard him scraping away with a match while the dog was scratching itself. Suddenly the match struck, and there was nothing to be seen or heard. Basil Basilich stared at me, and I stared at him. He asked me what all the nonsense was. I told him that if you made Socrates and Frederick the Great put their heads together over it, they couldn't explain it; and I told him all about it. He jumped out of bed like a scalded cat, and wanted to have his carriage called, to go away at once. I wanted to argue with him, but he only made more noise. He told me there must be some curse upon me, and that nothing would make him stay. I got him more or less quiet at last, but he insisted on having a bed in another room, and a light all night.

"When he was having his tea in the morning, he was calmer, and he gave me his advice to go away from home for some days, and then, perhaps, the thing would come to an end.

"He was a decidedly clever man, and I had great respect for his acumen. He got round his mother-in-law quite amazingly. He got her to accept letters of exchange, and she was as tame as a sheep. She made him commissioner for the administration of all her property. Fools don't do that sort of thing with their mothers-in-law. However, he was in a bad temper when he went away for I won a hundred more roubles from him, and he was cross. He told me I was behaving unthankfully towards him. How on earth could the luck be my fault? But I did as he advised, and I started for the town the same day. I knew an old man there who kept an inn, and who was a Dissenter, and it was to his house that I went. He was a little old creature, and a bit snappish, because he had lost his wife and all his children, and he was alone. He couldn't bear the smell of tobacco, and dogs were his particular horror. Rather than see a dog in his rooms he would have left the house. 'Behold,' he would say, 'the all-holy Virgin, who is graciously pleased to hang inside my room, and then how could I allow the unclean brutes to come sniffing in there.' Of course it is want of education. As far as I am concerned, I am content that everybody should use the common sense that God gives him. That's my Gospel."

"You seem to be a philosopher," said Anthony Stephanich, with the same smile as before.

Porphyry Capitonovich made a slight movement of the eyebrows, and also moved his moustache a little. He said:

"As to my being a philosopher, no proof has yet been adduced, but I teach philosophy to other people."

This made everybody look at Anthony Stephanich. We expected some startling reply, or at least a glance of scathing indignation. We were mistaken. The smile of the Ministerial Councillor changed from one of contempt to one of indifference. He yawned; he changed the position of his feet. There was nothing more.

"Well," said Capitonovich, "I took up my quarters in this old man's house; for the sake of his acquaintance with me, he put me in his own room, and made himself up a bed behind a screen. It wasn't a good room, at its best, and it was hot and stuffy beyond all belief. Everything was sticky, and the flies were all over the place. In one corner there was a cupboard full of old holy pictures covered with tarnished plates all bulging out. There was a smell of oil and drugs like a chemist's shop. There were two pillows on the bed, and black beetles ran out if you touched them. For want of something to do I drank more tea than I wanted, and then, beastly as the place was I got into bed. I could hear the old Dissenter on the other side of the screen sighing and groaning and mumbling his prayers. Then he went to sleep. It wasn't long before he began snoring. I listened to him. He began gently, and then it got worse and worse. I became irritated. It was a long time since I put out my own light, but it was not dark, because there was a lamp burning in front of the holy pictures. It was this that put me out. I got out of bed as quietly as I could, walked barefoot to the lamp, and blew it out. Nothing happened. So I thought it was all right, and got back into bed again. But I was hardly in before I heard the old story again. The dog was scratching and shaking himself—the whole thing as before. I lay still in bed, listening to see what would happen next. My landlord woke up. I heard him call out, 'Sir, what's the matter; have you put out the lamp, sir?' I made no answer, and I heard him get out of bed and say, 'What's the matter? What's the matter?—dog—dog—the d—d Niconian.' I called to him not to put himself out, but to come to me, as something very odd was happening. He emerged from behind his screen with the end of an unbleached wax taper in his hand. Such a figure I had never seen—his fierce eyes and hairy figure, with the hair growing even in his ears, were just like a badger. On his head he had a white felt hat; his white beard went down to his girdle, and over his chest he had a waistcoat with brass buttons. His feet were thrust into a pair of old furred slippers, and he diffused around him a pervading odour of gin. In this guise he proceeded to the holy pictures, before which he crossed himself three times with his two forefingers. Then he relighted the lamp, crossed himself again, and having done so, turned round to me, and said in a thick voice—

" 'Well, what's the matter?'

"I told him the whole story. He did not utter a syllable; he scratched his head. When I had done, he sat down, still silent, on the foot of my bed. Here he proceeded to scratch his stomach and the nape of his neck, and to rub himself. But still he never uttered a word. At last I said to him—

" 'Well, Theodoulos Ivanovich, I want to know what you think about it. Don't you think it's a temptation of the Evil One?'

"The old man looked at me.

" 'Temptation of the Evil One!' said he. 'You think that,

do you? It would be all very well in your own tobacco reek, but how about this house? This house is an holy place. A temptation of the Evil One? If it is not a temptation of the Evil One, what is it?'

"Then he sat silent, thinking and scratching himself. At last he said to me, though not very distinctly, because the hair got into his mouth—

" 'Go to Belev. There's only one man that I know of that can help you. He lives at Belev. He is one of our people. If he likes to help you, so much the better for you. If he does not like, you've got nothing more to do.'

"I asked him how I could find the man.

" 'I'll tell you,' said the Nonconformist, 'but, after all, why should it be a temptation of the Evil One? It's a vision; it may become even a revelation, but you're not up to all that. That's beyond you. Well, now, try to get to sleep, with God the Father and His Christ watching over you. I am going to burn some incense. We will think about it tomorrow. You know that second thoughts are almost always best.'

"In the morning, accordingly, we took counsel together, although he had nearly choked me in the night with his incense. The address which he gave me was this. When I got to Belev I was to go into the square and to ask at the second shop on the right hand for a certain Prochorovich, and give him a letter. The letter was a scrap of paper on which was written, 'In the Name of the Father, and of the Son, and of the Holy Ghost. Amen. To Sergius Prochorovich Pervoushine. Trust this man. Theodoulus Ivanovich. Send some cabbages, and praised be God's Holy Name.' I thanked my old Dissenter, and forthwith ordered a carriage, and went to Belev. My argument was, 'This thing in the night has not done me any harm yet, but it's very tiresome, and it's not the thing for a man like me or an officer.' What do you think?"

"And you went to Belev?" said Phinoplentoff.

"Yes, I went there straight. When I got to the square, I asked at the second shop on the right for Prochorovich. They told me he was not there. I asked where he lived, and they told me, in his own house in the suburb on the Oka. I accordingly crossed the Oka, and found the house in question, which might more fitly have been described as a shanty. I found a man in a darned blue shirt, with a torn cap, working among cabbages, with his back to me. I came up to him and said, 'Are you so and so?' He turned round, and I give you my word of honour, I never saw such a pair of eyes. He was old, he had no teeth, his face was as small as one's hand, and he had a beard like a he-goat.

" 'Yes,' he said, 'I am he. What can I do to serve you?'

" 'There,' said I, and gave him the letter.

"He stared hard at me, and then said—

" 'Be pleased to come into my room, I am not able to read without glasses.'

"We went into his room. It was a perfect kennel, bare and wretched, and with hardly space enough in which to turn round. On the wall there was a sacred picture, as black as coal, with black heads of Saints with gleaming whites to their eyes. He pulled out the drawer in an old table, took out a pair of spectacles mounted in iron, fixed them upon his nose and read the letter, after which he fixed his eyes on me through the spectacles.

" 'Have you need of me?'

" 'Yes.'

" 'Well, tell me what it is. I am listening.'

"He sat down, took out of his pocket an old checked pocket-handkerchief, full of holes, and spread it upon his knees. Me he never invited to sit down. He fixed upon me a look of power and dignity which might have become a Senator or a Minister of the Government. To my amazement I suddenly found myself seized with an emotion of terror. My heart seemed to sink within my shoes. Then he averted his gaze. This seemed to be enough, and when I had recovered myself a little, I told him my story. He said nothing, but frowned and bit his lips. Then, with an air of majesty and dignity, he slowly asked me my name, my age, who had been my parents, and whether I was married or single. After I told him this, he bit his lips and frowned again; then he held up one finger, and said, 'Cast yourself down before the holy images of the pure and helpful Saints, Sabbatius and Zosimus of the Solovetsky.'

"I threw myself down flat upon my face, and I might almost as well have remained lying there, such was the awe and fear with which this man inspired me. I would have done anything that he told me. Gentlemen, I see that you are laughing at me, but I assure you that I didn't feel anything like laughing. At last he said—

" 'Get up, sir, it is possible to help you. What has been sent to you is not a punishment, but a warning, that means to say that you are in danger, but, fortunately for you, there is some one praying for you. Go to the market-place and buy a young dog, keep it always with you both day and night; your visions will stop, and, moreover, you will find the dog useful.'

"Heaven seemed to open before me. His words filled me with gladness. I bowed profoundly to him, and was turning to go away when it struck me that I ought to give him something. I took out a three-rouble note, but he pushed it away with his hand and said:

" 'Give it to a chapel or to the poor; things like this are not paid for.'

"I bowed before him again, down to his very girdle, and walked off straight to the market-place. As I reached the shops, the first thing I saw was a man in a long grey gabardine, carrying a liver-coloured dog about two months old. I asked the man to stop and tell me the price of his dog. He said, 'Two roubles', and I proposed to give him three. He thought I was mad, but I gave him the bank-note to hold in his teeth while he carried the dog for me to my carriage. The coachman was soon ready, and I was at home the same evening. I kept the dog on my knees the whole time, and when he whined I called him my treasure. I gave him food and water, and had straw brought up to my room and made him a bed there. When I had blown the candle out and found myself in the dark, I wondered what was going to happen, but nothing happened. I began to feel quite bold, and called on the unseen power to begin its usual performance, but there was no response. Then I called in my servant and asked him if he could hear anything, but he could hear nothing either."

"Was that the end of it?" said Anthony Stephanich, but without sneering.

"It was the end of the noises," said Porphyry Capitonovich, "but it was not the end of the whole story. The dog grew, and became a large, strong setter. He showed an extraordinarily strong attachment to me. There is very little sport down in our part of the world, but whenever I took him out with me I always found it good. I used to take him all about with me. Sometimes he started a hare, or a partridge, or a wild duck, but he never went far from me. Wherever I went, he came too. I took him with me even when I went to bathe. A lady of my acquaintance wanted to turn him out of the drawing-room one day. We had a downright battle. I ended by breaking the affected creature's windows for her. Well, one fine day in summer there was the worst drought that I have ever known. There was a sort of haze in the air. Everything was burnt up. It was dark. The sun was like a red ball, and the dust was enough to make one sneeze. The earth gaped with cracks. I got tired of staying in the house, half-undressed, with shutters shut, and as it got a little cooler I made up my mind to go and call on a lady who lived about a verst off. She was a kind-hearted woman, still pretty young, and always smart. She was a little original, but that is rather an advantage in women than otherwise. I got to the steps of her door most frightfully thirsty, but I knew that Nymphodora Semenovna would pick me up with whortleberry-water and other refreshments. I had my hand on the door-handle, when I suddenly heard a tremendous row, and children shrieking, on the other side of a cottage, and in an instant a great red brute, that at first I did not see was a dog, made straight for me with his mouth open, his eyes red, and his hair all up. I had hardly gasped when it flew full at my chest. I almost had a fit. I shall never forget the white teeth and the foaming tongue close to my face. In an instant my own dog flew to my rescue like a flash of lightning, and hung on to the other's neck like a leech. The other one choked, snapped, and fell back. I opened the door, and jumped into the hall. I did not know where I was. I threw myself against a door with all my strength and yelled for help—while the two dogs fought upon the steps. The whole house was roused. Nymphodora ran out with her hair down. There was a lull in the noise, and I heard somebody call out to shut the gate. I peeped through the door. There was nothing on the steps, but men were running about the court seizing logs of wood as if they were mad themselves. I saw an old woman poke her cap out of a dormer window, and heard her call out that the dog had run down through the village, and I went out to look for mine. Presently he came into the court, limping, and hurt, and bloody. I asked what on earth was the matter, for there was a crowd gathered as if there had been a fire. They told me it was one of the Count's dogs that had gone mad, and that it had been about since the day before. This was a Count who was a neighbour of mine, and who had all sorts of strange dogs.

"I was in an awful fright, and I went to a looking-glass to see if I had got hurt. There was nothing, thank God, but I looked as green as grass, and Nymphodora Semenovna was lying on the sofa sobbing like a hen clucking. No wonder, too. It was her nerves, and her kind-heartedness. When she came to a little she said to me in a hollow voice—

" 'Are you still alive?'

" 'Yes,' I said, 'I am still alive. My dog saved me.' She said—

" 'What a noble thing! Did the mad dog kill him?'

" 'No,' said I, 'he is not killed, but he is very much hurt.'

"She answered, 'Then he ought to be shot at once.'

"I told her I would not. I was going to try to cure him.

"Then the dog himself came and scratched at the door, and I at once let him in.

" 'Oh, what are you doing?' she said, 'he will bite us all.'

"I said, 'Forgive me; it does not come out all at once like that.'

"She said, 'How can you? You have gone off your head.'

"I said, 'Nymphodora, do be quiet and talk sense,' but she called out to me to go away with my horrid dog.

"I said I was going to go.

"She said, 'Go away at once, don't stay a moment. Go away; you're a brute. Never you dare to see me again. I daresay you have got hydrophobia, too.'

"I said, 'All right, but just be good enough to let me have the carriage; there might be danger if I walked all the way back.'

"She stared at me. 'You can have the carriage or anything that you want, if only you will go away at once. Just look at its eyes.'

"She bolted out of the room, and hit one of the maids whom she met, and then I heard her taken ill next door. You can take it as what you like, but Nymphodora Semenovna and I were never friends again from that day onwards, and the more I think about it the more I feel that if it was for nothing else, I ought to be thankful for that to my dog to my dying day. I ordered the carriage and took the dog home with me in it. When I got home I examined him and washed his wounds. I thought the best thing I could do would be to take him next day to the wise man of the country. He was an astonishing old man. He mumbles something or other over water. Some people say he puts snakes' slime into it. He gives it you to drink, and it makes you all right at once. I thought that I would get myself bled at the same time. Bleeding is a good thing for fits. Of course you ought not to be bled in the arm, but in the dimple."

"Where is the dimple?" asked Phinoplentoff, timidly.

"Do you not know? It is the place under the hand, at the end of the thumb, where you put the snuff when you want to take a good lot of it. See. That is the right place to be bled, you can see that for yourself. The blood that comes out of the hand is the vein blood. In the other place it is the silly blood. Doctors don't know about those sort of things. The Germans know nothing about it. Farriers do it a great deal. They are very good at it. They just put their scissors there and give them a tap with the hammer, and the whole thing is done. The night came on while I was thinking about it, and it was time to go to bed. So I went, and of course, I kept the dog with me; but I don't know whether it was the heat or the shock that I had had, or the fleas, or what I was thinking about, but I could not get to sleep. I got restless. I drank water, I opened the window. I got the guitar and played the Moujik of Koumarino with Italian variations. But it would not do. I thought it was the room that I could not stand, so I took a pillow and two sheets and a coverlet and went across the garden, and made myself a bed in the hay under the shed. I was more comfortable there. It was a calm night. Every now and then there was a little breath of air that touched you on the face, like a woman's hand. The fresh hay smelt good, like tea. The crickets sang in the apple trees. Every now and then you'd hear a hen quail clucking, and you felt that she was happy in the dew beside her mate. The sky was quite still. The stars were shining, and there were little light clouds, like flakes of cotton wool, that hardly changed.

"Well," continued Porphyry Capitonovich, "I lay down, but I didn't get to sleep. I kept thinking, and especially about presentiments, and what that man Prochorovich had said to me, when he told me to look out for squalls, and now how such an extraordinary thing had happened. I could not understand it. It was impossible to understand it. All of a sudden the dog jumped up and whined. I thought his wounds were hurting him. Then the moon kept me awake. Do you not believe me? I assure you it did. The moon was straight in front of me, round, and flat, and big, and yellow, and I thought that she was there to tease me. I put out my tongue at her. Did she want to know what I was thinking about? I turned over, but I felt her upon my ear, and upon the back of my neck. It was like rain all over me. I opened my eyes again. The moon showed every little point of grass, every little twig in the hay, every little spider's web, as if it was cut out sharp, and she said, 'There you are, look at it.' There was nothing more to be done. I rested my head upon my hand and looked. I have strong eyes and I could not sleep. The gate of the shed was wide open and I looked through. One could see the country for five versts. It was patchy, clear in some places and dark in others, as is the case in moonlight. I was looking out over it when I thought I saw something moving a long distance off. Then I saw something pass quickly much nearer. Then I saw a dark figure leap. It had come much nearer then. I wondered if it was a hare. I supposed so, and it was coming nearer. Then I saw it was bigger than a hare. It came out of the shadow on to the meadow, which lay quite white in the moonlight, and the thing moved upon it like a great black spot. Evidently it was some kind of wild beast—a fox, perhaps, or a wolf. My heart began to beat. But what was there to be afraid of? There are plenty of beasts that run about at night. My curiosity overcame my fear. I got up and rubbed my eyes, when all of a sudden I turned cold as if ice had been put down my back. The shadowy creature grew larger and darted in at the gate of the yard. I then saw that it was an enormous brute with a great head. It shot past like a bullet, then stopped and began to snuff. It was the mad dog. I could neither move nor cry. It bounded in at the door of the shed with sparkling eyes, howled, and leaped upon me as I lay upon the hay. At that moment my own dog sprang forward wide-awake. The two beasts fought and fell. I don't remember what followed. I only remember that I fell over them somehow in a heap, escaped through the garden, and got to my own bedroom. When I recovered myself a little, I woke up the whole house, and we all armed ourselves and sallied out. I got a sword and a revolver. I had bought the revolver just after the emancipation of the serfs, for reasons which I need not mention, and a bad one it was. I missed two shots out of every three. We went to the shed with burning sticks; we went forward and shouted, but we could not hear anything. At last we went in, and there we found my dog lying dead and the other disappeared.

"'I am not ashamed to tell you that I cried like a child.

"I knelt down and kissed the body of the poor beast who had saved my life twice, and I was there still when my old housekeeper Prascovia came and said to me, 'What's the matter with you? To get into such a state about a dog. God forgive you. You ought to be ashamed of yourself, and you'll catch cold.' It is true I had hardly anything on. 'If the dog has got killed to save your life, it is an honour for him.' I did not agree with Prascovia, but I went back to the house. As to the mad dog, it was shot by a soldier the next day, which must have been providential, as the soldier had never fired off a gun before, although he possessed a medal for having been one of the saviours of the country in 1812. Now, gentlemen, that is why I told you that something supernatural had once happened to me."

With these words, Porphyry Capitonovich was silent and filled his pipe. We all looked at one another without speaking. At last Phinoplentoff said, "No doubt you lead an holy life, and this is a reward"—but here he stopped short, for he saw that Porphyry got red in the face.

"But if you once admit the existence of the supernatural," said Anthony Stephanich, "and that it can enter into the ordinary affairs of every-day life, allow me to ask what scope is left for the exercise of reason?"

Nobody had anything to answer.

THE HOUND OF DEATH

by Agatha Christie

THE WORLD-FAMOUS CREATOR *of Hercule Poirot and Miss Marples scarcely requires an introduction —yet so great is Agatha Christie's reputation as a writer of brilliantly intriguing detective plots that her equally effective stories of supernatural horror are almost entirely overlooked. Hopefully the inclusion of this story will help bring about greater recognition of Miss Christie's forays into the genre of the occult.*

I

It was from William P. Ryan, American newspaper correspondent, that I first heard of the affair. I was dining with him in London on the eve of his return to New York and happened to mention that on the morrow I was going down to Folbridge.

He looked up and said sharply: "Folbridge, Cornwall?"

Now only about one person in a thousand knows that there is a Folbridge in Cornwall. They always take it for granted that the Folbridge, Hampshire, is meant. So Ryan's knowledge aroused my curiosity.

"Yes," I said. "Do you know it?"

He merely replied that he was darned. He then asked if I happened to know a house called Trearne down there.

My interest increased.

"Very well indeed. In fact, it's to Trearne I'm going. It's my sister's house."

"Well," said William P. Ryan. "If that doesn't beat the band!"

I suggested that he should cease making cryptic remarks and explain himself.

"Well," he said. "To do that I shall have to go back to an experience of mine at the beginning of the war."

I sighed. The events which I am relating took place in 1921. To be reminded of the war was the last thing any man wanted. We were, thank God, beginning to forget . . . Besides, William P. Ryan on his war experiences was apt, as I knew, to be unbelievably long-winded.

But there was no stopping him now.

"At the start of the war, as I dare say you know, I was in Belgium for my paper—moving about some. Well, there's a little village—I'll call it X. A one-horse place if there ever was one, but there's quite a big convent there. Nuns in white what do you call 'em—I don't know the name of the order. Anyway, it doesn't matter. Well, this little burgh was right in the way of the German advance. The Uhlans arrived—"

I shifted uneasily. William P. Ryan lifted a hand reassuringly.

"It's all right," he said. "This isn't a German atrocity story. It might have been, perhaps, but it isn't. As a matter of fact, the boot's on the other leg. The Huns made for that convent— they got there and the whole thing blew up."

"Oh!" I said, rather startled.

"Odd business, wasn't it? Of course, offhand, I should say the Huns had been celebrating and had monkeyed round with their own explosives. But it seems they hadn't anything of that kind with them. They weren't the high explosive johnnies. Well, then, I ask you, what should a pack of nuns know about high explosive? Some nuns, I should say!"

"It is odd," I agreed.

"I was interested in hearing the peasants' account of the matter. They'd go it all cut and dried. According to them it was a slap-up one hundred per cent efficient first class modern miracle. It seems one of the nuns had got something of a reputation—a budding saint—went into trances and saw visions. And according to them she worked the stunt. She called down the lightning to blast the impious Hun—and it blasted him all right

—and everything else within range. A pretty efficient miracle, that!

"I never really got at the truth of the matter--hadn't time. But miracles were all the rage just then—angels at Mons and all that. I wrote up the thing, put in a bit of sob stuff, and pulled the religious stop out well, and sent it to my paper. It went down very well in the States. They were liking that kind of thing just then.

"But (I don't know if you'll understand this) in writing, I got kinder interested. I felt I'd like to know what really had happened. There was nothing to see at the spot itself. Two walls still left standing, and on one of them was a black powder mark that was the exact shape of a great hound. The peasants round about were scared to death of that mark. They called it the Hound of Death and they wouldn't pass that way after dark.

"Superstition's always interesting. I felt I'd like to see the lady who worked the stunt. She hadn't perished, it seemed. She'd gone to England with a batch of other refugees. I took the trouble to trace her. I found she'd been sent to Trearne, Folbridge, Cornwall."

I nodded.

"My sister took in a lot of Belgian refugees the beginning of the war. About twenty."

"Well, I always meant, if I had time, to look up the lady. I wanted to hear her own account of the disaster. Then, what with being busy and one thing and another, it slipped my memory. Cornwall's a bit out of the way anyhow. In fact, I'd forgotten the whole thing till your mentioning Folbridge just now brought it back."

"I must ask my sister," I said. "She may have heard something about it. Of course, the Belgians have all been repatriated long ago."

"Naturally. All the same, in case your sister does know anything I'll be glad if you'd pass it on to me."

"Of course I will," I said heartily.

And that was that.

2

It was the second day after my arrival at Trearne that the story recurred to me. My sister and I were having tea on the terrace.

"Kitty," I said, "didn't you have a nun among your Belgians?"

"You don't mean Sister Marie Angelique, do you?"

"Possibly I do," I said cautiously. "Tell me about her."

"Oh! my dear, she was the most uncanny creature. She's still here, you know."

"What? In the house?"

"No, no, in the village. Dr Rose—you remember Dr Rose?"

I shook my head.

"I remember an old man of about eighty-three."

"Dr Laird. Oh! he died. Dr Rose has only been here a few years. He's quite young and very keen on new ideas. He took the most enormous interest in Sister Marie Angelique. She has hallucinations and things, you know, and apparently is most frightfully interesting from a medical point of view. Poor thing, she'd nowhere to go—and really was in my opinion quite potty —only impressive, if you know what I mean—well, as I say, she'd nowhere to go, and Dr Rose very kindly fixed her up in the village. I believe he's writing a monograph or whatever it is that doctors write, about her."

She paused and then said.

"But what do you know about her?"

"I heard a rather curious story."

I passed on the story as I had received it from Ryan. Kitty was very much interested.

"She looks the sort of person who could blast you—if you know what I mean," she said.

"I really think," I said, my curiosity heightened, "that I must see this young woman."

"Do. I'd like to know what you think of her. Go and see Dr Rose first. Why not walk down to the village after tea?"

I accepted the suggestion.

I found Dr Rose at home and introduced myself. He seemed a pleasant young man, yet there was something about his personality that repelled me. It was too forceful to be altogether agreeable.

The moment I mentioned Sister Marie Angelique he stiffened to attention. He was evidently keenly interested. I gave him Ryan's account of the matter.

"Ah!" he said thoughtfully. "That explains a great deal."

He looked up quickly at me and went on.

"The case is really an extraordinarily interesting one. The woman arrived here having evidently suffered some severe mental shock. She was in a state of great mental excitement also. She was given to hallucinations of a most startling character. Her personality is most unusual. Perhaps you would like to come with me and call upon her. She is really well worth seeing."

I agreed readily.

We set out together. Our objective was a small cottage on the outskirts of the village. Folbridge is a most picturesque place. It lies in the mouth of the river Fol mostly on the east bank, the west bank is too precipitous for building, though a few cottages do cling to the cliffside there. The doctor's own cottage was perched on the extreme edge of the cliff on the west side. From it you looked down on the big waves lashing against the black rocks.

The little cottage to which we were now proceeding lay inland out of the sight of the sea.

"The district nurse lives here," explained Dr Rose. "I have arranged for Sister Marie Angelique to board with her. It is just as well that she should be under skilled supervision."

"Is she quite normal in her manner?" I asked curiously.

"You can judge for yourself in a minute," he replied, smiling.

The district nurse, a dumpy pleasant little body, was just setting out on her bicycle when we arrived.

"Good evening, nurse, how's your patient?" called out the doctor.

"She's much as usual, doctor. Just sitting there with her

hands folded and her mind far away. Often enough she'll not answer when I speak to her, though for the matter of that it's little enough English she understands even now."

Rose nodded, and as the nurse bicycled away, he went up to the cottage door, rapped sharply and entered.

Sister Marie Angelique was lying in a long chair near the window. She turned her head as we entered.

It was a strange face—pale, transparent looking, with enormous eyes. There seemed to be an infinitude of tragedy in those eyes.

"Good evening, my sister," said the doctor in French.

"Good evening, M. le docteur."

"Permit me to introduce a friend, Mr Anstruther."

I bowed and she inclined her head with a faint smile.

"And how are you today?" inquired the doctor, sitting down beside her.

"I am much the same as usual." She paused and then went on. "Nothing seems real to me. Are they days that pass—or months—or years? I hardly know. Only my dreams seem real to me."

"You still dream a lot, then?"

"Always—always—and, you understand?—the dreams seem more real than life."

"You dream of your own country—of Belgium?"

She shook her head.

"No. I dream of a country that never existed—never. But you know this, M. le docteur. I have told you many times." She stopped and then said abruptly: "But perhaps this gentleman is also a doctor—a doctor perhaps for the diseases of the brain?"

"No, no." Rose was reassuring, but as he smiled I noticed how extraordinarily pointed his canine teeth were, and it occurred to me that there was something wolf-like about the man. He went on:

"I thought you might be interested to meet Mr Anstruther. He knows something of Belgium. He has lately been hearing news of your convent."

Her eyes turned to me. A faint flush crept into her cheeks.

"It's nothing, really," I hastened to explain. "But I was dining the other evening with a friend who was describing the ruined walls of the convent to me."

"So it was ruined!"

It was a soft exclamation, uttered more to herself than to us. Then looking at me once more she asked hesitatingly: "Tell me, Monsieur, did your friend say how—in what way—it was ruined?"

"It was blown up," I said, and added: "The peasants are afraid to pass that way at night."

"Why are they afraid?"

"Because of a black mark on a ruined wall. They have a superstitious fear of it."

She leaned forward.

"Tell me, Monsieur—quick—quick—tell me! What is that mark like?"

"It has the shape of a huge hound," I answered. "The peasants call it the Hound of Death."

"Ah!"

A shrill cry burst from her lips.

"It is true then—it is true. All that I remember is true. It is not some black nightmare. It happened! It happened!"

"What happened, my sister?" asked the doctor in a low voice.

She turned to him eagerly.

"*I remembered.* There on the steps, I remembered. I remembered the way of it. I used the power as we used to use it. I stood on the altar steps and I bade them to come no farther. I told them to depart in peace. They would not listen, they came on although I warned them. And so—" she leaned forward and made a curious gesture. "And so I loosed the Hound of Death on them . . ."

She lay back on her chair shivering all over, her eyes closed.

The doctor rose, fetched a glass from a cupboard, half-filled it with water, added a drop or two from a little bottle which he produced from his pocket, then took the glass to her.

"Drink this," he said authoritatively.

She obeyed—mechanically as it seemed. Her eyes looked far away as though they contemplated some inner vision of her own.

"But then it is all true," she said. "Everything. The City of the Circles, the People of the Crystal—everything. It is all true."

"It would seem so," said Rose.

His voice was low and soothing, clearly designed to encourage and not disturb her train of thought.

"Tell me about the City," he said. "The City of Circles, I think you said?"

She answered absently and mechanically.

"Yes—there were three circles. The first circle for the chosen, the second for the priestesses and the outer circle for the priests."

"And in the centre?"

She drew her breath sharply and her voice sank to a tone of indescribable awe.

"The House of the Crystal . . ."

As she breathed the words, her right hand went to her forehead and her finger traced some figure there.

Her figure seemed to grow more rigid, her eyes closed, she swayed a little—then suddenly she sat upright with a jerk, as though she had suddenly awakened.

"What is it?" she said confusedly. "What have I been saying?"

"It is nothing," said Rose. "You are tired. You want to rest. We will leave you."

She seemed a little dazed as we took our departure.

"Well," said Rose when we were outside. "What do you think of it?"

He shot a sharp glance sideways at me.

"I suppose her mind must be totally unhinged," I said slowly.

"It struck you like that?"

"No—as a matter of fact, she was—well, curiously convincing. When listening to her I had the impression that she actually had done what she claimed to do—worked a kind of gigantic miracle. Her belief that she did so seems genuine enough. That is why—"

"That is why you say her mind must be unhinged. Quite so. But now approach the matter from another angle. Supposing that she did actually work that miracle—supposing that she did, personally, destroy a building and several hundred human beings."

"By the mere exercise of will?" I said with a smile.

"I should not put it quite like that. You will agree that one person could destroy a multitude by touching a switch which controlled a system of mines."

"Yes, but that is mechanical."

"True, that is mechanical, but it is, in essence, the harnessing and controlling of natural forces. The thunderstorm and the power house are, fundamentally, the same thing."

"Yes, but to control the thunderstorm we have to use mechanical means."

Rose smiled.

"I am going off at a tangent now. There is a substance called wintergreen. It occurs in nature in vegetable form. It can also be built by man synthetically and chemically in the laboratory."

"Well?"

"My point is that there are often two ways of arriving at the same result. Ours is, admittedly, the synthetic way. There might be another. The extraordinary results arrived at by Indian fakirs, for instance, cannot be explained away in any easy fashion. The things we call supernatural are not necessarily supernatural at all. An electric flashlight would be supernatural to a savage. The supernatural is only the natural of which the laws are not yet understood."

"You mean?" I asked, fascinated.

"That I cannot entirely dismiss the possibility that a human being *might* be able to tap some vast destructive force and use it to further his or her ends. The means by which this was accomplished might seem to us supernatural—but would not be so in reality."

I stared at him.

He laughed.

"It's a speculation, that's all," he said lightly. "Tell me, did you notice a gesture she made when she mentioned the House of the Crystal?"

"She put her hand to her forehead."

"Exactly. And traced a circle there. Very much as a Catholic makes the sign of the cross. Now, I will tell you something rather interesting, Mr Anstruther. The word crystal having occurred so often in my patient's rambling, I tried an experiment. I borrowed a crystal from someone and produced it unexpectedly one day to test my patient's reaction to it."

"Well?"

"Well, the result was very curious and suggestive. Her whole body stiffened. She stared at it as though unable to believe her eyes. Then she slid to her knees in front of it, murmured a few words—and fainted."

"What were the few words?"

"Very curious ones. She said: 'The Crystal! Then the Faith still lives!'"

"Extraordinary!"

"Suggestive, is it not? Now the next curious thing. When she came round from her faint she had forgotten the whole thing. I showed her the crystal and asked her if she knew what it was. She replied that she supposed it was a crystal such as fortune tellers used. I asked her if she had ever seen one before? She replied: 'Never, M. le docteur.' But I saw a puzzled look in her eyes. 'What troubles you, my sister?' I asked. She replied: 'Because it is so strange. I have never seen a crystal before and yet—it seems to me that I know it well. There is something—if only I could remember . . .' The effort at memory was obviously so distressing to her that I forbade her to think any more. That was two weeks ago. I have purposely been biding my time. Tomorrow, I shall proceed to a further experiment."

"With the crystal?"

"With the crystal. I shall get her to gaze into it. I think the result ought to be interesting."

"What do you expect to get hold of?" I asked curiously.

The words were idle ones but they had an unlooked-for result. Rose stiffened, flushed, and his manner when he spoke had changed insensibly. It was more formal, more professional.

"Light on certain mental disorders imperfectly understood. Sister Marie Angelique is a most interesting study."

So Rose's interest was purely professional? I wondered.

"Do you mind if I come along too?" I asked.

It may have been my fancy, but I thought he hesitated before he replied. I had a sudden intuition that he did not want me.

"Certainly. I can see no objection."

He added:

"I suppose you're not going to be down here very long?"

"Only till the day after tomorrow."

I fancied that the answer pleased him. His brow cleared and he began talking of some recent experiments carried out on guinea pigs.

3

I met the doctor by appointment the following afternoon, and we went together to Sister Marie Angelique. Today, the doctor was all geniality. He was anxious, I thought, to efface the impression he had made the day before.

"You must not take what I said too seriously," he observed, laughing. "I shouldn't like you to believe me a dabbler in occult sciences. The worst of me is I have an infernal weakness for making out a case."

"Really?"

"Yes, and the more fantastic it is, the better I like it."

He laughed as a man laughs at an amusing weakness.

When we arrived at the cottage, the district nurse had something she wanted to consult Rose about, so I was left with Sister Marie Angelique.

I saw her scrutinizing me closely. Presently she spoke.

"The good nurse here, she tells me that you are the brother of the kind lady at the big house where I was brought when I came from Belgium?"

"Yes," I said.

"She was very kind to me. She is good."

She was silent, as though following out some train of thought. Then she said:

"M. le docteur, he too is a good man?"

I was a little embarrassed.

"Why, yes. I mean—I think so."

"Ah!" She paused and then said: "Certainly he has been very kind to me."

"I'm sure he has."

She looked up at me sharply.

"Monsieur—you—you who speak to me now—do you believe that I am mad?"

"Why, my sister, such an idea never—"

She shook her head slowly—interrupting my protest.

"Am I mad? I do not know—the things I remember—the things I forget . . ."

She sighed, and at that moment Rose entered the room.

He greeted her cheerily and explained what he wanted her to do.

"Certain people, you see, have a gift for seeing things in a crystal. I fancy you might have such a gift, my sister."

She looked distressed.

"No, no, I cannot do that. To try to read the future—that is sinful."

Rose was taken aback. It was the nun's point of view for which he had not allowed. He changed his ground cleverly.

"One should not look into the future. You are quite right. But to look into the past—that is different."

"The past?"

"Yes—there are many strange things in the past. Flashes come back to one—they are seen for a moment—then gone again. Do not seek to see anything in the crystal since that is not allowed you. Just take it in your hands—so. Look into it— look deep. Yes—deeper—deeper still. You remember, do you not? You remember. You hear me speaking to you. You can answer my questions. Can you not hear me?"

Sister Marie Angelique had taken the crystal as bidden, handling it with a curious reverence. Then, as she gazed into it, her eyes became blank and unseeing, her head drooped. She seemed to sleep.

Gently the doctor took the crystal from her and put it on the table. He raised the corner of her eyelid. Then he came and sat by me.

"We must wait till she wakes. It won't be long, I fancy."

He was right. At the end of five minutes, Sister Marie Angelique stirred. Her eyes opened dreamily.

"Where am I?"

"You are here—at home. You have had a little sleep. You have dreamt, have you not?"

She nodded.

"Yes, I have dreamt."

"You have dreamt of the Crystal?"

"Yes."

"Tell us about it."

"You will think me mad, M. le docteur. For see you, in my dream, the Crystal was a holy emblem. I even figured to myself a second Christ, a Teacher of the Crystal who died for his faith, his followers hunted down—persecuted . . . But the faith endured."

"The faith endured?"

"Yes—for fifteen thousand full moons—I mean, for fifteen thousand years."

"How long was a full moon?"

"Thirteen ordinary moons. Yes, it was in the fifteenth thousand full moon—of course, I was a Priestess of the Fifth Sign in the House of the Crystal. It was in the first days of the coming of the Sixth Sign . . ."

Her brows drew together, a look of fear passed over her head.

"Too soon," she murmured. "Too soon. A mistake . . . Ah! yes, I remember! The Sixth Sign!"

She half sprang to her feet, then dropped back, passing her hand over her face and murmuring:

"But what am I saying? I am raving. These things never happened."

"Now don't distress yourself."

But she was looking at him in anguished perplexity.

"M. le docteur, I do not understand. Why should I have these dreams—these fancies? I was only sixteen when I entered the religious life. I have never travelled. Yet I dream of cities, of strange people, of strange customs. Why?" She pressed both hands to her head.

"Have you ever been hypnotized, my sister? Or been in a state of trance?"

"I have never been hypnotized, M. le docteur. For the other, when at prayer in the chapel, my spirit has often been caught up from my body, and I have been as one dead for many hours. It was undoubtedly a blessed state, the Reverend Mother said— a state of grace. Ah! yes," she caught her breath. *"I remember, we too called it a state of grace."*

"I would like to try an experiment, my sister." Rose spoke in a matter-of-fact voice. "It may dispel those painful half-recollections. I will ask you to gaze once more in the crystal. I will then say a certain word to you. You will answer with another. We will continue in this way until you become tired. Concentrate your thoughts on the crystal, not upon the words."

As I once more unwrapped the crystal and gave it into Sister Marie Angelique's hands, I noticed the reverent way her hands touched it. Reposing on the black velvet, it lay between her slim palms. Her wonderful deep eyes gazed into it. There was a short silence, and then the doctor said: *"Hound."*

Immediately Sister Marie Angelique answered *"Death."*

I do not propose to give a full account of the experiment. Many unimportant and meaningless words were purposely introduced by the doctor. Other words he repeated several times, sometimes getting the same answer to them, sometimes a different one.

4

That evening in the doctor's little cottage on the cliffs we discussed the result of the experiment.

He cleared his throat, and drew his notebook closer to him.

"These results are very interesting—very curious. In answer to the words 'Sixth Sign', we get variously *Destruction, Purple, Hound, Power*, then again *Destruction*, and finally *Power*. Later, as you may have noticed, I reversed the method, with the following results. In answer to *Destruction*, I get *Hound*; to *Purple*, *Power*; to *Hound*, *Death* again, and to *Power*, *Hound*. That all holds together, but on a second repetition of *Destruction*, I get *Sea*, which appears utterly irrelevant. To the words 'Fifth Sign', I get *Blue, Thoughts, Bird, Blue* again, and finally the rather suggestive phrase *Opening of mind to mind*. From the fact that 'Fourth Sign' elicits the word *Yellow*, and later *Light*, and that 'First Sign' is answered by *Blood*, I deduce that each Sign had a particular colour, and possibly a particular symbol, that of the Fifth Sign being a *bird*, and that of the Sixth a *hound*. However, I surmise that the Fifth Sign represented what is familiarly known as telepathy—the opening of mind to mind. The Sixth Sign undoubtedly stands for the Power of Destruction."

"What is the meaning of *Sea*?"

"That I confess I cannot explain. I introduced the word later and got the ordinary answer of *Boat*. To Seventh Sign I got first *Life*, the second time *Love*. To Eighth Sign, I got the answer *None*. I take it therefore that Seven was the sum and number of the signs."

"But the Seventh was not achieved," I said on a sudden inspiration. "Since through the Sixth came *Destruction*!"

"Ah! You think so? But we are taking these—mad ramblings very seriously. They are really only interesting from a medical point of view."

"Surely they will attract the attention of psychic investigators."

The doctor's eyes narrowed. "My dear sir, I have no intention of making them public."

"Then your interest?"

"Is purely personal. I shall make notes on the case, of course."

"I see." But for the first time I felt, like the blind man, that I didn't see at all. I rose to my feet.

"Well, I'll wish you goodnight, doctor. I'm off to town again tomorrow."

"Ah!" I fancied there was satisfaction, relief perhaps, behind the exclamation.

"I wish you good luck with your investigations," I continued lightly. "Don't loose the Hound of Death on me next time we meet!"

His hand was in mine as I spoke, and I felt the start it gave. He recovered himself quickly. His lips drew back from his long pointed teeth in a smile.

"For a man who loved power, what a power that would be!" he said. "To hold every human being's life in the hollow of your hand!"

And his smile broadened.

5

That was the end of my direct connection with the affair.

Later, the doctor's notebook and diary came into my hands. I will reproduce the few scanty entries in it here, though you will understand that it did not really come into my possession until some time afterwards.

Aug. 5th. Have discovered that by "the Chosen", Sister M.A. means those who reproduced the race. Apparently they were held in the highest honour, and exalted above the Priesthood. Contrast this with early Christians.

Aug. 7th. Persuaded Sister M.A. to let me hypnotize her. Succeeded in inducing hypnotic sleep and trance, but no *rapport* established.

Aug. 9th. Have there been civilizations in the past to which ours is as nothing? Strange if it should be so, and I the only man with the clue to it . . .

Aug. 12th. Sister M.A. not at all amenable to suggestion when hypnotized. Yet state of trance easily induced. Cannot understand it.

Aug. 13th. Sister M.A. mentioned today that in "state of grace" the "gate must be closed, lest another should command the body". Interesting—but baffling.

Aug. 18th. So the First Sign is none other than ... (*words erased here*) ... then how many centuries will it take to reach the Sixth? But if there should be a short-cut to Power ...

Aug. 20th. Have arranged for M.A. to come here with Nurse. Have told her it is necessary to keep patient under morphia. Am I mad? Or shall I be the Superman, with the Power of Death in my hands?

(*Here the entries cease*)

6

It was, I think, on August 29th that I received the letter. It was directed to me, care of my sister-in-law, in a sloping foreign handwriting. I opened it with some curiosity. It ran as follows:

CHER MONSIEUR.—I have seen you but twice, but I have felt that I could trust you. Whether my dreams are real or not, they have grown clearer of late ... And, Monsieur, one thing at all events, the Hound of Death is no dream ... In the days I told you of (whether they are real or not, I do not know) He Who was Guardian of the Crystal revealed the Sixth Sign to the People too soon ... Evil entered into their hearts. They had the power to slay at will—and they slew without justice—in anger. They were drunk with the lust of Power. When we saw this, We who were yet pure, we knew that once again we should not complete the Circle and come to the Sign of Everlasting Life. He who would have been the next Guardian of the Crystal was bidden to act. That the old might die, and the new, after endless ages, might come again, *he loosed the Hound of Death upon the sea* (being careful not to close the circle), and the sea rose up in the shape of a Hound and swallowed the land utterly . . .

Once before I remembered this—*on the altar steps in Belgium* . . .

The Dr Rose, he is of the Brotherhood. He knows the First Sign, and the form of the Second, though its meaning is hidden to all save a chosen few. *He would learn of me the Sixth.* I have withstood him so far—but I grow weak. Monsieur, it is not well that a man should come to power before his time. Many centuries must go by ere the world is ready to have the power of death delivered into its hand . . . I beseech you, Monsieur, you who love goodness and truth, to help me . . . before it is too late.

> Your sister in Christ,
> MARIE ANGELIQUE

I let the paper fall. The solid earth beneath me seemed a little less solid than usual. Then I began to rally. The poor woman's belief, genuine enough, had almost affected *me*! One thing was clear. Dr Rose, in his zeal for a case, was grossly abusing his professional standing. I would run down and—

Suddenly I noticed a letter from Kitty amongst my other correspondence. I tore it open.

"Such an awful thing has happened," I read. "You remember Dr Rose's little cottage on the cliff? It was swept away by a landslide last night, and the doctor and that poor nun, Sister Marie Angelique, were killed. The *débris* on the beach is too awful—all piled up in a fantastic mass—from a distance it looks like a great *hound* . . ."

The letter dropped from my hand.

The other facts may be coincidence. A Mr Rose, whom I discovered to be a wealthy relative of the doctor's, died suddenly that same night—it was said struck by lightning. As far as was known no thunderstorm had occurred in the neighbourhood, but one or two people declared they had heard one peal of thunder. He had an electric burn on him "of a curious shape". His will left everything to his nephew, Dr Rose.

Now, supposing that Dr Rose succeeded in obtaining the secret of the Sixth Sign from Sister Marie Angelique. I had always felt him to be an unscrupulous man—he would not shrink at taking his uncle's life if he were sure it could not be brought home to him. But one sentence of Sister Marie Angelique's letter rings in my brain: ". . . being careful not to close the Circle . . ." Dr Rose did not exercise that care—was perhaps unaware of the steps to take, or even of the need for them. So the Force he employed returned, completing its circuit . . .

But of course it is all nonsense! Everything can be accounted for quite naturally. That the doctor believed in Sister Marie Angelique's hallucinations merely proves that *his* mind, too, was slightly unbalanced.

Yet sometimes I dream of a continent under the seas where men once lived and attained to a degree of civilization far ahead of ours . . .

Or did Sister Marie Angelique remember *backwards*—as some say is possible—and is this City of the Circles in the future and not the past?

Nonsense—of course the whole thing was mere hallucination!

DEAD DOG

by Manly Wade Wellman

FOR MORE THAN *forty years, Manly Wade Wellman has been writing first-class stories of science fiction, fantasy and terror. His best-known novel,* Who Fears the Devil?, *considered by many to be a classic of fantastic literature, was recently filmed as* The Legend of Hillbilly John, *and a sturdy collection of his best short stories has just been published under the title of* Worse Things Waiting. *Mr. Wellman also has a reputation as a distinguished expert on American folklore and superstitions. In the North Carolina mountains where he lives, devil-hounds are said to roam: "One has three legs only, and to see it in the twilight is a sure warning of bad luck, maybe death. So I don't go looking for it."*

Manly Wade Wellman was born in the Portuguese West African village of Kamundongo where his father was a medical missionary. "Probably my whole bent for tales of supernatural terror started there," writes Mr Wellman, "where wise old men sat and told of such things and everyone believed." Told and believed in this way was the story of the Dead Dog . . .

Dead dogs may bite the careless feet.—*Umbundu proverb.*

They brought the rebel chief Kaflatala out of the jungle to Father Labossier's mud-brick house, brought him in a *tepoia* because he still limped from a Portuguese bullet in his thigh. Twenty black warriors, clicking their spears respectfully, followed the hammock-litter and formed a row outside the stockade as Kaflatala dismounted and hobbled up the path.

Springing from his seat on the porch, Father Labossier walked swiftly to meet his old friend. The chief was lean, taller by a head than the sturdy priest, and black as basalt save for a grey scar across his proud face from eye to nostril. The two men said the requisite *Kalungu* greetings and sat on a log under the broad-leafed fig-tree. Then Kaflatala spoke:

"Your advice came to me in my hiding. I cannot hope to win against the Portuguese soldiers; now I must surrender and save my people further punishment."

"That is wise, Kaflatala," nodded Father Labossier, smiling. Nine years in west Africa had not dulled the missionary zeal that had stirred him from a pleasant curé of souls near Antwerp, and moments like this repaid him for long toil. "The white man's Saviour, of whom I told you," he continued, "will make your sentence a light one."

The scar darkened on Kaflatala's face and his wide lips tightened. "My people will suffer no more, that is all. Rodriguez, the Portuguese captain, will kill me."

The priest held up a hand in protest. "Not all Portuguese are cruel. It is true that Captain Rodriguez's heart is sick; he was sent here because he had sinned against the laws at home—"

"However he came here, he will kill me." Kaflatala fairly jerked out the words, then apologized for interrupting. "Goodbye, my father. We shall meet again."

Still Father Labossier argued. "A power will save you, Kaflatala."

"A power may avenge me," was the bleak reply. "That is all."

Father Labossier brought notebook and pencil from his pocket and scribbled a note as he sat.

"This asks that you be treated kindly," he explained. "My fastest servant will bear it to the fort ahead of you."

The chief thanked him courteously, and rose. "One favour before I go."

"Name it."

Kaflatala emitted a chirping whistle. At once something black and swift sped from behind the row of warriors, dashed through the gate and up the path—a huge, shaggy hound, as black as thunder. It was as large as a calf, and its eyes shone with an uneasy greenish pallor. Yet it seemed gentle, thrusting its long, ugly head under the chief's hand.

"Will you keep my dog for me?" asked Kaflatala.

"Until you come back," agreed Father Labossier.

"I do not come back," insisted the other, and Father Labossier changed the subject by asking how the beast was called.

"Ohondongela," replied the master.

That word means "revenge" in the Umbundu, and Father Labossier, eyeing the dog, thought it as fierce as its name. Black, rough, lean, powerful of jaw and long of fang, it had something of the forbidding wild about it, almost like a forest beast; but all dogs were once forest beasts, at the beginning of time . . .

Kaflatala again excused himself for cutting the visit short, spoke commandingly to Ohondongela, and smiled when the brute curled himself obediently at the feet of Father Labossier. Then he stumped to the gate, crept into his *tepoia* and gave the signal for the march to continue.

Three days later Father Labossier was wakened before dawn by the dismal howling of Kaflatala's hound. He grumbled sleepily, then reflected that a man of God must not think unkindly, even of a beast. He rose, took an early breakfast, pottered among the lettuces in his garden and at noon read a marriage service over a giggling young couple that wanted white man's magic for good luck in its new household. Afterwards he wrote letters to a favourite nephew, to a group of fellow-priests at home, and to the Dutch trader who sent him supplies from Benguela. At about four o'clock in the afternoon a chorus of shouts from his servants betokened a stranger coming up the trail.

It was a runner, bare-legged and wearing a faded khaki shirt, who advanced to the porch, saluted in clumsy military fashion, and offered a parcel sewn in rice-sacking.

"From the fort," the runner told him. "Captain Rodriguez has sent it."

"Thank you." Some answer, of course, to his plea for mercy to Kaflatala. But why a package and no letter? There must be a note inside.

Producing a clasp-knife, the priest ripped the sacking.

A face looked up at him through the ragged hole—a black, dead face. Upon it a pallid grey scar ran from eye to nostril. Kaflatala had been right; Captain Rodriguez had made short work of him, and thus was answering Father Labossier's recommendations of mercy.

Again rose the doleful wail of Ohondongela the hound. And just before sunset the great beast lay down and died, quietly, quickly and inexplicably.

Three moons had waned and waxed again, and the same runner from the fort met Father Labossier just outside his stockade. It was mid-afternoon, as on the runner's previous appearance, and again he had something from Captain Rodriguez—not a package this time, but a letter.

The priest took the envelope and gazed for a moment at the almost indecipherable characters that spelled his own name upon it. They had been set down by a shaking hand, a hand that he knew as the captain's. He had written to Rodriguez on the same day that he had received Kaflatala's head; he had stiffly indicted the officer as a cruel and cowardly murderer, and had sent a duplicate of the letter to the governor at Loanda. Nobody had replied—was this a belated acknowledgment of his message, perhaps a justification of Rodriguez's action or a further sneer at the priest?

He opened the letter and read it, his kindly face spreading over with wonder. For Rodriguez was praying for help and comfort in the name of Christian mercy and priestly compassion. The last phrase, in particular, was out of character: "I know I have sinned, yet ask for the aid I do not deserve."

The priest lifted his eyes to the waiting runner. "Go back and say that I will come tomorrow."

The native paused, embarrassed, then replied diffidently that his master was in dreadful case and that there was no white doctor to do magic for his healing. Could not Father Labossier come at once?

"It will be an all-night trek," demurred the priest. Then he thought better of his hesitancy, and added, "But a moon will shine. I shall go with you."

He changed into flannel shirt, walking-boots and a wide hat. Upon his shoulder he slung a canteen and a musette with medicines. In his pocket were prayer-book and Bible. From his little arsenal he chose a hunting-rifle, for lions might be hunting along the night trail. Then, placing his oldest servant in charge of the house, he set off with the man from the fort.

It was a wearying tramp by moonlight, and an eventful one. At sunrise he came to the fort, where, brooding in his quarters over untasted food, Captain Rodriguez waited for him.

Father Labossier was shocked at sight of the Portuguese. When they had last met, four months previously, Rodriguez had been florid, swaggering, vigorous. Now he sagged shrunkenly inside his dirty white uniform. The face he lifted was pale, its eyes wild, and his once-jaunty moustache drooped.

"Father," he mumbled hoarsely, "I am ridden by devils."

Father Labossier took the captain's hand. It trembled in his grasp. "I do not doubt you, my son," he replied gravely. "Yours has been an evil life."

Rodriguez grimaced in doleful acceptance of the reproof. "Come, let us sit down in the porch—in the blessed moonlight."

Outside, they took canvas chairs. Rodriguez sighed as if in exhaustion, gazed for a moment across the bare drill-ground towards the barracks of the native soldiers. Then:

"My sins crouch beside my bed at night."

The priest waited for a moment. When his companion did not continue, he said tentatively: "Seek forgiveness from the Lord."

"If I could!" Rodriguez leaned towards him, and his breath in Father Labossier's face was the breath of a sick man. "A

Christian God cannot be invoked—only a savage devil, to spare me."

Father Labossier fingered the silver cross that hung from his neck. "That thought is a transgression, my son. Unsay it."

The captain clutched his face in wasted hands and his shoulders shook, as with sobs. Finally he forced himself to speak of what lay upon his soul.

Three nights before, he had retired, as usual, to his lonely bedchamber. He spoke of his habitual preparations; the examination of the windows to see if their gratings and mosquito nets were in place, his locking of the door against possible night prowlers, his placing of a service pistol beside the water glass on his bedside table. Nothing untoward had happened during the day; it had been even tiresome. His thoughts before slumber had taken the form of an idle review of his work and a wistful consideration of his chances to be forgiven certain indiscretions and called home to Portugal. Then he had dozed off, to wake suddenly and in fear.

At this point in his narrative, he hid his face again and shuddered uncontrollably. Father Labossier laid a hand on the captain's arm, and strength flowed from him into that shaken frame.

"I looked towards the window, and there I saw it. Blood of the saints, I saw it! By the window—a great dog!"

"Dog!" repeated the other, leaning forward in his turn. "What sort of a dog?"

"Large—black and shaggy. It was sitting up, and its head and shoulders rose above the window-sill, making a silhouette against the moonlight. Its eyes, like green lamps of hell, stared at me. The hate in them!" Captain Rodriguez's face twitched with the memory.

"I see. And then?"

"I screamed, a thing I have not done since I was a baby. A moment later, my orderly was pounding and calling at the door; and the dog—had gone."

"Gone!" echoed the priest.

"Yes, vanished like a candle-flame snuffed."

Father Labossier clicked his tongue. "Was it not a dream, that?"

Captain Rodriguez laughed, but not merrily. He had thought that very thing, he admitted, though he was too nervous to sleep any more that night. In the morning he had forced himself to forget the adventure and had gone about his duties with a heart that grew lighter as the day progressed. By nightfall the nervousness returned, and he lulled himself to sleep with a bromide.

"Again—mark me, Father—again I saw to windows, mosquito netting, lock. I put from me the troublesome vision of the night before. I slept."

Father Labossier took a cigar from his pocket. "The dream—"

"It was no dream, I say. When does a dream come twice in two nights?" The captain's lips twitched, showing teeth that were set as though to hold back a dreadful pain. "The dog returned. I woke in sudden instinctive fear, and there it was as before. No, not as before."

"What do you mean?" asked Father Labossier, biting the end of his cigar.

"It had been at the window the first time. Now it was at the foot of my bed, nearer to me by half the floor's width." Rodriguez laid his fist to his lips, as though to crush their trembling. "It was so large as to look over the footboard at me. Its green eyes burned into mine."

Father Labossier said, very quietly, that a real dog could not have looked Rodriguez in the eye.

"No, and this was no real dog. It was my gaze that faltered, and I screamed aloud."

"As before?"

"Yes, as before. And my orderly came, bearing a light that shed itself through the cracks of the door. At that beam, the thing was gone, completely and instantly. I rose to let the orderly in—never have I allowed a native to see me so upset."

Father Labossier rubbed a match on the sole of his boot. "And then, my son?"

"In the morning I sent for you. But last night, while you were on the trail—last night, the dreadful dog from hell visited me yet again!"

He flung out a hand, palm vertical. "No farther away than that, it sat at my side. It breathed upon me, I heard the growl in its throat. And somehow I snatched up the pistol from my table and fired into its face—it vanished. But tonight—*it will not vanish!*"

His voice had risen to a wail. Again the priest's strong, steady hand clutched his companion's quivering one, calming the frantic shivers.

"You have fancied these things, my son."

"But I swear they are true, by every saint in the calendar. Come, Father, to my room. You shall see for yourself."

Still murmuring set phrases of comfort, Father Labossier followed Rodriguez back into the house. The captain's sleeping-compartment was comfortable and even luxurious beyond military requirements, appointed as he had described.

"See," urged Rodriguez, laying an unsteady finger upon the door-jamb. "This round hole—my bullet made it."

"I see it," Father Labossier assured him.

"And you observe the gratings and nets at the window? The lock on my door? Well, then—"

Father Labossier cleared his throat. He was well-read, and something of an amateur psychologist. "My son, you knew, perhaps, that Chief Kaflatala had a great black hound."

"Did he? I never saw it."

"You had heard, perhaps, of the beast. Its name was Ohondongela."

Rodriguez bit his lips. "Ohondongela—revenge." He calmed himself and said that he might have heard of it.

"Ah, then," said Father Labossier, "it has become a symbol with you, my son, of the wrong your heart's core has admitted."

Much more he said, drawing upon Freud and the gospels in turn. Captain Rodriguez listened carefully, nodding from time to time as though he comprehended the argument and was disposed to agree.

"But if this is the truth," he said when the priest had made an end, "what am I to do?"

"You have begun by repenting and confessing," Father Labossier told him. "Tonight—"

"Tonight!" gasped Rodriguez, turning pale.

"Do not fear. Go to bed as usual, composing yourself. I shall sit up in the parlour. If the dream returns, call me—softly. We will deal with it together."

Rodriguez drew a deep breath, as of relief. "I am hungry," he said suddenly. "You, Father, have not breakfasted. Forgive me my neglect, and be my guest."

Towards nightfall Captain Rodriguez became nervous, meditative and boastful by turns. Once he spoke on native magic and twice of charms against the devil. Again, forgetting his abject admission of wrong, he loudly argued that he was justified in executing Kaflatala. He invited Father Labossier to drink with him and, when the priest refused, drank by himself. He drank entirely too much, and picked up his guitar to sing the sun down with a gay ballad. But as dusk fell he turned solemn once more and threw the instrument aside.

"Father," he muttered, "are you sure all will be well?"

"I am sure of nothing," Father Labossier felt obliged to reply. "I am very hopeful; that is all."

Rodriguez lifted his shoulders, but the shrug ended in a shiver. "Let me sit up with you," he begged. "We will talk."

"We have already talked. The best way to solve this evil is to face it."

Some time later the captain drank yet more, said good-night and went into his bedroom.

Sitting alone in the parlour, Father Labossier examined the bookshelf. It bore several weighty works on military science and tactics, and a row of Portuguese novels. From among these he selected *Rhum Azul*, by Ernest Souza. As he scanned the first page he sighed with relish. It was a mystery-adventure tale, and

Father Labossier, though devout, was not disdainful of such fare. Indeed, after the Scriptures and the writings of the saints, he enjoyed best Edgar Allan Poe, Maurice Leblanc and the *Adventures of Sherlock Holmes.* This story would help him while away the hours. He savoured a chapter, a second, a third . . .

The calm night tore open before a blood-banishing scream of fear and agony.

Dropping the book, Father Labossier sprang to his feet. In three quick strides he crossed to the door of Rodriguez's bedroom. Even as he reached it, the scream rose higher, died suddenly, and a spatter of pistol shots rang out. Then a second voice, inhuman and savage, the jabbering snarl of a beast at the kill—

The door was locked. Father Labossier shook the knob futilely, then turned as a native orderly rushed in from the rear of the house. Together they flung their shoulders against the panel. A second time. The lock gave, the door drove in. The orderly paused to catch up a lamp, and the priest stepped across the threshold.

He shrank back, staring into the gloom. Something dark and hunched was squirming violently upon the bed. Then, as the orderly lifted the light above Father Labossier's shoulder, that shape was gone.

The two men stared and wondered. The gratings and nets were in place. Nowhere along the tight walls could even a beetle find entrance or exit.

But Captain Rodriguez lay still among the tumbled sheets. His throat had been ripped out to the neckbone. One hand clutched his revolver, the other a tuft of shaggy black hair— such hair as had grown upon Ohondongela, the long-dead hound of the long-dead Kaflatala.

THE DUTCH OFFICER'S STORY

by Catherine Crowe

CATHERINE CROWE *(1800–1871) was a Victorian novelist and dramatist whose most successful novel* Susan Hopley *(1841) was favourably compared to the work of Sir Walter Scott. A self-confessed disciple of the Scottish mystic George Combe, she became deeply interested in psychic phenomena, collecting together apparently authenticated ghost stories into a series of enthralling volumes that helped make the reading and telling of ghost stories one of the most popular of Victorian pastimes. The Dutch Officer's Story is from* Ghosts and Family Legends *(1859).*

"Well, I think nothing can be so cowardly as to be afraid to own the truth," said the pretty Madame de B., an Englishwoman, who had married a Dutch officer of distinction.

"Are you really venturing to accuse the General of cowardice?" said Madame L.

"Yes," said Madame de B., "I want him to tell Mrs Crowe a ghost story—a thing that he saw himself—and he pooh-poohs it, though he owned it to me before we were married, and since too, saying that he never could have believed such a thing if he had not seen it himself."

While the wife was making this little *tirade*, the husband looked as if she was accusing him of picking somebody's pocket —*il perdait contenance* quite. "Now, look at him," she said, "don't you see guilt in his face, Mrs Crowe?"

"Decidedly," I answered; "so experienced a seeker of ghost stories as myself cannot fail to recognize the symptoms. I always find that when the circumstances is mere hearsay, and happened to nobody knows who, people are very ready to tell it; when it has happened to one of their own family, they are considerably less communicative, and will only tell it under protest; but when they are themselves the parties concerned, it is the most difficult thing imaginable to induce them to relate the thing seriously, and with its details; they say they have forgotten it, and don't believe it; and as an evidence of their incredulity, they affect to laugh at the whole affair. If the General will tell me the story, I shall think it quite as decisive a proof of courage as he ever gave in the field."

Betwixt bantering and persuasion, we succeeded in our object, and the General began as follows:

"You know the Belgian Rebellion (he always called it so) took place in 1830. It broke out at Brussels on August 28th, and we immediately advanced with a considerable force to attack that city; but as the Prince of Orange hoped to bring the people to reason, without bloodshed, we encamped at Vilvorde, whilst he entered Brussels alone, to hold a conference with the armed people. I was a Lieutenant-Colonel then, and commanded the 20th foot, to which regiment I had been lately appointed.

"We had been three or four days in cantonment, when I heard two of the men, who were digging a little drain at the back of my tent, talking of Jokel Falck, a private in my regiment, who was noted for his extraordinary disposition to somnolence. One of them remarked that he would certainly have got into trouble for being asleep on his post the previous night, if it had not been for Mungo. 'I don't know how many times he has saved him,' added he.

"To which the other answered that Mungo was a very valuable friend, and had saved many a man from punishment.

"This was the first time I had ever heard of Mungo, and I rather wondered who it was they alluded to; but the conversation slipped from my mind and I never thought of asking anybody.

"Shortly after this I was going my rounds, being field-officer of the day, when I saw by the moonlight the sentry at one of the outposts stretched upon the ground. I was some way off when I first perceived him, and I only knew what the object was from the situation, and because I saw the glitter of his accoutrements; but almost at the same moment that I discovered him, I observed a large black Newfoundland dog trotting towards him. The man rose as the dog approached, and had got upon his legs before I reached the spot. This occupied the space of about two minutes—perhaps, not so much.

" 'You were asleep on your post,' I said; and turning to the mounted orderly that attended me, I told him to go back and bring a file of the guard to take him prisoner, and to send a sentry to relieve him.

" 'Non, mon colonel,' said he, and from the way he spoke I perceived he was intoxicated, 'it's all the fault of that *damné* Mungo. Il m'a manqué.'

"But I paid no attention to what he said and rode on, concluding *Mungo* was some slang term of the men for drink.

"Some evenings after this, I was riding back from my brother's quarter—he was in the 15th, and was stationed about a mile from us—when I remarked the same dog I had seen before, trot up to a sentry who, with his legs crossed, was leaning against a wall. The man started, and began walking backwards and forwards on his beat. I recognized the dog by a large white streak on his side—all the rest of his coat being black.

"When I came up to the man, I saw it was Jokel Falck, and although I could not have said he was asleep, I strongly suspected that that was the fact.

" 'You had better take care of yourself, my man,' said I. 'I have half a mind to have you relieved, and make a prisoner of you. I believe I should have found you asleep on your post, if that dog had not roused you.'

"Instead of looking penitent, as was usual on these occasions, I saw a half smile on the man's face, as he saluted me.

" 'Whose dog is that?' I asked my servant, as I rode away.

" 'Je ne sais pas, mon Colonel,' he answered, smiling too.

"On the same evening at mess, I heard one of the subalterns say to the officer who sat next to him, 'It's a fact, I assure you, and they call him Mungo.'

" 'That's a new name they've got for Schnapps, isn't it?' I said.

" 'No sir; it's the name of a dog,' replied the young man, laughing.

" 'A black Newfoundland, with a large white streak on his flank?'

" 'Yes, sir, I believe that is the description,' replied he, tittering still.

" 'I have seen that dog two or three times,' said I. 'I saw him this evening—who does he belong to?'

" 'Well, sir, that is a difficult question,' answered the lad; and I heard his companion say, 'To Old Nick, I should think.'

" 'Do you mean to say you've really seen Mungo?' said somebody at the table.

" 'If Mungo is a large Newfoundland—black, with a white streak on its side—I saw him just now. Who does he belong to?'

"By this time, the whole mess table was in a titter, with the exception of one old captain, a man who had been years in the regiment. He was of very humble extraction, and had risen by merit to his present position.

" 'I believe Captain T. is better acquainted with Mungo than anybody present,' answered Major R., with a sneer. 'Perhaps he can tell you who he belongs to.'

"The laughter increased, and I saw there was some joke, but not understanding what it meant, I said to Captain G., 'Does the dog belong to Jokel Falck?'

" 'No, sir,' he replied, 'the dog belongs to nobody now. He once belonged to an officer called Joseph Atveld.'

" 'Belonging to this regiment?'

" 'Yes, sir.'

" 'He is dead, I suppose?'

" 'Yes, sir, he is.'

" 'And the dog has attached himself to the regiment?'

" 'Yes, sir.'

"During this conversation, the suppressed laughter continued, and every eye was fixed on Captain T., who answered me shortly, but with the utmost gravity.

" 'In fact,' said the major, contemptuously, 'according to Captain T., Mungo is the ghost of a deceased dog.'

"This announcement was received with shouts of laughter, in which I confess I joined, whilst Captain T. still retained an unmoved gravity.

" 'It is easier to laugh at such a thing than to believe it, sir,' said he. '*I* believe it, because I know it.'

"I smiled, and turned the conversation.

"If anybody at the table except Captain T. had made such an assertion as this, I should have ridiculed them without mercy; but he was an old man, and from the circumstances I have mentioned regarding his origin, we were careful not to offend him; so no more was said about Mungo, and in the hurry of events that followed, I never thought of it again. We marched on to Brussels the next day; and after that, had enough to do till we went to Antwerp, where we were besieged by the French the following year.

"During the siege, I sometimes heard the name of Mungo again; and one night, when I was visiting the guards and sentries as grand rounds, I caught a glimpse of him, and I felt sure that the man he was approaching when I observed him had been asleep; but he was screened by an angle of the bastion, and by the time I turned the corner, he was moving about.

"This brought to my mind all I had heard about the dog; and as the circumstance was curious, in any point of view, I mentioned what I had seen to Captain T. the next day, saying, 'I saw your friend Mungo, last night.'

" 'Did you, sir?' said he. 'It's a strange thing. No doubt, the man was asleep!'

" 'But do you seriously mean to say that you believe this to be a visionary dog, and not a dog of flesh and blood?'

" 'I do, sir; I have been quizzed enough about it; and, once or twice, have nearly got into a quarrel, because people will persist in laughing at what they know nothing about; but as sure as that is a sword you hold in your hand, so sure is that dog a spectre, or ghost—if such a word is applicable to a four-footed beast!'

" 'But it's impossible!' I said. 'What reason have you for such an extraordinary belief?'

" 'Why, you know, sir, man and boy I have been in the regiment all my life. I was born in it. My father was pay-sergeant of No. 3 company when he died; and I have seen Mungo myself, perhaps twenty times, and known, positively, of others seeing him twice as many more.'

" 'Very possibly; but that is no proof that it is not some dog that has attached himself to the regiment.'

" 'But I have seen and heard of the dog for fifty years, sir; and my father before me, had seen and heard of him as long!'

" 'Well, certainly, that is extraordinary—if you are sure of it, and that it's the same dog.'

" 'It's a remarkable dog, sir. You won't see another like it with that large white streak on his flank. He won't let one of our sentries be found asleep, if he can help; unless, indeed, the fellow is drunk. He seems to have less care of drunkards, but Mungo has saved many a man from punishment. I was once not a little indebted to him myself. My sister was married out of the regiment, and we had had a bit of a festivity, and drank rather too freely at the wedding, so that when I mounted guard that night—I wasn't to say, drunk, but my head was a little gone, or so; and I should have been caught nodding; but Mungo, knowing, I suppose, that I was not an habitual drunkard, woke me just in time.'

" 'How did he wake you?' I asked.

" 'I was roused by a short, sharp bark, that sounded close to my ears. I started up, and had just time to catch a glimpse of Mungo before he vanished.'

" 'Is that the way he always wakes the men?'

" 'So they say; and, as they wake, he disappears.'

"I recollected now that on each occasion when I had observed the dog, I had, somehow, lost sight of him in an instant; and, my curiosity being awakened, I asked Captain T. if ours were the only men he took charge of, or whether he showed the same attention to those of other regiments.

" 'Only the 20th, sir; the tradition is that after the battle of

Fontenoy, a large black mastiff was found lying beside a dead officer. Although he had a dreadful wound from a sabre cut on his flank, and was much exhausted from loss of blood, he would not leave the body; and even after we buried it, he could not be enticed from the spot. The men, interested by the fidelity and attachment of the animal, bound up his wounds, and fed and tended him; and he became the dog of the regiment. It is said that they had taught him to go his rounds before the guards and sentries were visited, and to wake any men that slept. How this may be, I cannot say; but he remained with the regiment till his death, and was buried with all the respect they could show him. Since that, he has shown his gratitude in the way I tell you, and of which you have seen some instances.'

" 'I suppose the white streak is the mark of the sabre cut. I wonder you never fired at him.'

" 'God forbid, sir, I should do such a thing,' said Captain T., looking sharp round at me. 'It's said that a man did so once, and that he never had any luck afterwards; that may be a superstition, but I confess I wouldn't take a good deal to do it.'

" 'If, as you believe, it's a spectre, it could not be hurt, you know; I imagine ghostly dogs are impervious to bullets.'

" 'No doubt, sir; but I shouldn't like to try the experiment. Besides, it would be useless, as I am convinced already.'

"I pondered a good deal upon this conversation with the old captain. I had never for a moment entertained the idea that such a thing was possible. I should have as much expected to meet the minotaur or a flying dragon as a ghost of any sort, especially the ghost of a dog; but the evidence here was certainly startling. I had never observed anything like weakness and credulity about T.; moreover, he was a man of known courage, and very much respected in the regiment. In short, so much had his earnestness on the subject staggered me that I resolved whenever it was my turn to visit the guards and sentries that I would carry a pistol with me ready primed and loaded, in order to settle the question. If T. was right, there would be an interesting fact established, and no harm done; if, as I could not help suspecting, it was a cunning trick of the men who had trained this dog to wake them, while they kept up the farce of the spectre, the animal would be well out of the way, since their reliance on him no doubt led them to give way to drowsiness when they would otherwise have struggled against it. Indeed, though none of our men had been detected—thanks, perhaps, to Mungo—there had been so much negligence lately in the garrison that the general had issued very severe orders on the subject.

"However, I carried my pistol in vain; I did not happen to fall in with Mungo; and some time afterwards, on hearing the thing alluded to at the mess-table, I mentioned what I had done, adding, 'Mungo is too knowing, I fancy, to run the risk of getting a bullet in him.'

" 'Well,' said Major R., 'I should like to have a shot at him, I confess. If I thought I had any chance of seeing him, I'd certainly try it; but I've never seen him at all.'

" 'Your best chance," said another, 'is when Jokel Falck is on duty. He is such a sleepy scoundrel that the men say if it was not for Mungo he'd pass half his time in the guard house.'

" 'If I could catch him I'd put an ounce of lead into him; that he may rely on.'

" 'Into Jokel Falck, sir?' said one of the subs, laughing.

" 'No, sir,' replied Major R., 'into Mungo—and I'll do it, too.'

" 'Better not, sir,' said Captain T., gravely; provoking thereby a general titter round the table.

"Shortly after this, as I was one night going to my quarter, I saw a mounted orderly ride in and call out a file of the guard to take a prisoner.

" 'What's the matter?' I asked.

" 'One of the sentries asleep on his post, sir; I believe it's Jokel Falck.'

" 'It will be the last time, whoever it is,' I said, 'for the general is determined to shoot the next man that's caught.'

" 'I should have thought Mungo had stood Jokel Falck's friend so often that he'd never have allowed him to be caught,' said the adjutant. 'Mungo has neglected his duty.'

" 'No, sir,' said the orderly, gravely. 'Mungo would have waked him, but Major R. shot at him.'

" 'And killed him,' I said.

" 'The man made no answer, but touched his cap and rode away.

"I heard no more of the affair that night; but the next morning, at a very early hour, my servant woke me, saying that Major R. wished to speak to me. I desired he should be admitted, and the moment he entered the room I saw by his countenance that something serious had occurred; of course, I thought the enemy had gained some unexpected advantage during the night, and sat up in bed inquiring eagerly what had happened.

"To my surprise he pulled out his pocket-handkerchief and burst into tears. He had married a native of Antwerp, and his wife was in the city at this time. The first thing that occurred to me was that she had met with some accident, and I mentioned her name.

" 'No, no,' he said; 'my son, my boy, my poor Fritz!'

"You know that in our service, every officer first enters his regiment as a private soldier, and for a certain space of time does all the duties of that position. The major's son, Fritz, was thus in his noviciate. I concluded he had been killed by a stray shot, and for a minute or two I remained in this persuasion, the major's speech being choked by his sobs. The first words he uttered were—

" 'Would to God I had taken Captain T.'s advice!'

" 'About what?' I said. 'What has happened to Fritz?'

" 'You know,' said he, 'yesterday I was field officer of the day; and when I was going my rounds last night, I happened to ask my orderly, who was assisting to put on my sash, what men we had told off for the guard. Amongst others, he named Jokel Falck, and remembering the conversation the other day at the mess table, I took one of my pistols out of the holster and, after loading, put it in my pocket. I did not expect to see the dog, for I had never seen him; but as I had no doubt that the story of the spectre was some dodge of the men, I determined if ever I did to have a shot at him. As I was going through the

Place de Meyer, I fell in with the general, who joined me, and we rode on together, talking of the siege. I had forgotten all about the dog, but when we came to the rampart, above the Bastion du Matte, I suddenly saw exactly such an animal as the one described, trotting beneath us. I knew there must be a sentry immediately below where we rode, though I could not see him, and I had no doubt that the animal was making towards him; so without saying a word, I drew out my pistol and fired, at the same moment jumping off my horse, in order to look over the bastion, and get a sight of the man. Without comprehending what I was about, the general did the same, and there we saw the sentry lying on his face, fast asleep.'

" 'And the body of the dog?' said I.

" 'Nowhere to be seen,' he answered, 'and yet I must have hit him—I fired bang into him. The general says it must have been a delusion, for he was looking exactly in the same direction and saw no dog at all—but I am certain I saw him, so did the orderly.'

" 'It was Fritz—Fritz was the sentry,' said the major, with a fresh burst of grief. The courtmartial sits this morning, and my boy will be shot, unless interest can be made with the general to grant him a pardon.'

"I rose and dressed myself immediately, but with little hope of success. Poor Fritz being the son of an officer, was against him rather than otherwise—it would have been considered an act of favouritism to spare him. He was shot; his poor mother died of a broken heart, and the major left the service immediately after the surrender of the city."

"And have you ever seen Mungo again?" said I.

"No," he replied; "but I have heard of others seeing him."

"And are you convinced that it was a spectre, and not a dog of flesh and blood?"

"I fancy I was then—but, of course, one can't believe—"

"Oh, no," I rejoined. "Oh, no; never mind the facts, if they don't fit into our theories."

VENDETTA

by Guy de Maupassant

ALTHOUGH AGED ONLY forty-three when he died, Guy de Maupassant (1850–1893) wrote sufficient in his brief lifetime to fill thirty thick volumes and to establish a permanent reputation as one of France's greatest story-tellers. Influenced at the outset by Flaubert and Zola, his work was realistic in approach, yet his own darkly pessimistic vision, nurtured on fears of impending madness, easily lent itself to the occasional supernatural story such as The Horla *and to tales of fatalism and violent irony of which* Vendetta *is a superb example.*

Palo Saverini's widow dwelt alone with her son in a small, mean house on the ramparts of Bonifacio. Built on a spur of the mountain and in places actually overhanging the sea, the town looks across the rock-strewn Straits to the low-lying coast of Sardinia. On the other side, girdling it almost completely, there is a fissure in the cliff, like an immense corridor, which serves as a port, and down this long channel, as far as the first houses, sail the small Italian and Sardinian fishing-boats, and once a fortnight the broken-winded old steamer from Ajaccio. Clustered together on the white hillside, the houses form a patch of even more dazzling whiteness. Clinging to the rock, gazing down upon those deadly Straits where scarcely a ship ventures, they look like the nests of birds of prey. The sea and the barren coast, stripped of all but a scanty covering of grass, are forever harassed by a restless wind, which sweeps along the narrow funnel, ravaging the banks on either side. In all directions the black points of innumerable rocks jut out from the water, with trails of white foam streaming from them, like torn shreds of cloth, floating and quivering on the surface of the waves.

The widow Saverini's house was planted on the very edge of the cliff, and its three windows opened upon this wild and dreary prospect. She lived there with her son Antoine and their dog Sémillante, a great gaunt brute of the sheep-dog variety, with a long, rough coat, whom the young man took with him when he went out shooting.

One evening, Antoine Saverini was treacherously stabbed in a quarrel by Nicolas Ravolati, who escaped that same night to Sardinia.

At the sight of the body, which was brought home by passers-by, the old mother shed no tears, but she gazed long and silently at her dead son. Then, laying her wrinkled hand upon the corpse, she promised him the Vendetta. She would not allow anyone to remain with her, and shut herself up with the dead body. The dog Sémillante, who remained with her, stood at the foot of the bed and howled, with her head turned towards her master and her tail between her legs. Neither of them stirred, neither the dog nor the old mother, who was now leaning over the body, gazing at it fixedly, and silently shedding great tears. Still wearing his rough jacket, which was pierced and torn at the breast, the boy lay on his back as if asleep, but there was blood all about him, on his shirt, which had been stripped off in order to expose the wound, on his waistcoat, trousers, face and hands. His beard and hair were matted with clots of blood.

The old mother began to talk to him, and at the sound of her voice the dog stopped howling.

"Never fear, never fear, you shall be avenged, my son, my little son, my poor child. You may sleep in peace. You shall be avenged, I tell you. You have your mother's word, and you know she never breaks it."

Slowly she bent down and pressed her cold lips to the dead lips of her son.

Sémillante resumed her howling, uttering a monotonous, long-drawn wail, heart-rending and terrible. And thus the two remained, the woman and the dog, till morning.

The next day Antoine Saverini was buried, and soon his name ceased to be mentioned in Bonifacio.

He had no brother, nor any near male relation. There was no man in the family who could take up the vendetta. Only his mother, his old mother, brooded over it.

From morning till night she could see, just across the Straits, a white speck upon the coast. This was the little Sardinian village of Longosardo, where the Corsican bandits took refuge whenever the hunt for them grew too hot. They formed almost the entire population of the hamlet. In full view of their native shores they waited for a chance to return home and regain the bush. She knew that Nicolas Ravolati had sought shelter in that village.

All day long she sat alone at her window gazing at the opposite coast and thinking of her revenge, but what was she to do with no one to help her, and she herself so feeble and near her end? But she had promised, she had sworn by the dead body of her son, she could not forget, and she dared not delay. What was she to do? She could not sleep at night, she knew not a moment of rest or peace, but racked her brains unceasingly. Sémillante asleep at her feet, would now and then raise her head and emit a piercing howl. Since her master had disappeared, this had become a habit, it was as if she were calling him, as if she, too, were inconsolable and preserved in her canine soul an ineffaceable memory of the dead.

One night, when Sémillante began to whine, the old mother had an inspiration of savage, vindictive ferocity. She thought about it till morning. At daybreak she rose and betook herself to church. Prostrate on the stone floor, humbling herself before God, she besought Him to aid and support her, to lend to her poor, worn-out body the strength she needed to avenge her son.

Then she returned home. In the yard stood an old barrel with one end knocked in, in which was caught the rain-water from the eaves. She turned it over, emptied it, and fixed it to the ground with stakes and stones. Then she chained up Sémillante to this kennel and went into the house.

With her eyes fixed on the Sardinian coast, she walked rest-
lessly up and down her room. He was over there, the murderer.

The dog howled all day and all night. The next morning
the old woman brought her a bowl of water, but no food, neither
soup nor bread. Another day passed. Sémillante was worn out
and slept. The next morning her eyes were gleaming, and her
coat standing, and she tugged frantically at her chain. And again
the old woman gave her nothing to eat. Maddened with hunger,
Sémillante barked hoarsely. Another night went by.

At daybreak, the widow went to a neighbour and begged for
two trusses of straw. She took some old clothes that had belonged
to her husband, stuffed them with straw to represent a human
figure, and made a head out of a bundle of old rags. Then, in
front of Sémillante's kennel, she fixed a stake in the ground and
fastened the dummy to it in an upright position.

The dog looked at the straw figure in surprise and, although
she was famished, stopped howling.

The old woman went to the pork butcher and bought a long
piece of black pudding. When she came home she lighted a
wood fire in the yard, close to the kennel, and fried the black
pudding. Sémillante bounded up and down in a frenzy, foaming
at the mouth, her eyes fixed on the gridiron with its maddening
smell of meat.

Her mistress took the steaming pudding and wound it like a
tie round the dummy's neck. She fastened it on tightly with
string as if to force it inwards. When she had finished she un-
chained the dog.

With one ferocious leap, Sémillante flew at the dummy's
throat and with her paws on its shoulders began to tear it. She
fell back with a portion of her prey between her jaws, sprang at
it again, slashing at the string with her fangs, tore away some
scraps of food, dropped for a moment, and hurled herself at it
in renewed fury. She tore away the whole face with savage
rendings and reduced the neck to shreds.

Motionless and silent, with burning eyes, the old woman
looked on. Presently she chained the dog up again. She starved
her another two days, and then put her through the same strange

performance. For three months she accustomed her to this method of attack, and to tear her meals away with her fangs. She was no longer kept on the chain. At a sign from her mistress, the dog would fly at the dummy's throat.

She learned to tear it to pieces even when no food was concealed about its throat. Afterwards as a reward she was always given the black pudding her mistress had cooked for her.

As soon as she caught sight of the dummy, Sémillante quivered with excitement and looked at her mistress, who would raise her finger and cry in a shrill voice, "Tear him."

One Sunday morning when she thought the time had come, the widow Saverini went to Confession and Communion, in an ecstasy of devotion. Then she disguised herself like a tattered old beggar man, and struck a bargain with a Sardinian fisherman, who took her and her dog across to the opposite shore.

She carried a large piece of black pudding wrapped in a cloth bag. Sémillante had been starved for two days and her mistress kept exciting her by letting her smell the savoury food.

The pair entered the village of Longosardo. The old woman hobbled along to a baker and asked for the house of Nicolas Ravolati. He had resumed his former occupation, which was that of a joiner, and he was working alone in the back of his shop.

The old woman threw open the door and called:

"Nicolas! Nicolas!"

He turned round. Slipping the dog's lead, she cried:

"Tear him! Tear him!"

The maddened dog flew at his throat. The man flung out his arms, grappled with the brute and they rolled on the ground together. For some moments he struggled, kicking the floor with his feet. Then lay still, while Sémillante tore his throat to shreds.

Two neighbours seated at their doors, remembered to have seen an old beggar man emerge from the house and, at his heels, a lean black dog, which was eating as it went along, some brown substance that its master was giving it.

By the evening the old woman had reached home again.

That night she slept well.

DOG OR DEMON?

by Theo Gift

THEO GIFT WAS *the pseudonym of Dora Havers (1847–1923), a prolific Victorian novelist and writer of children's stories. She is probably best remembered as the author of* Cape Town Dicky; Or, Colonel Jack's Boy, *a once-popular book for children.*

Dora Havers wrote one volume of weird stories, Not For the Night-time *(1889), from which this grim tale is taken.*

"The following pages came into my hands shortly after the writer's death. He was a brother officer of my own, had served under me with distinction in the last Afghan campaign, and was a young man of great spirit and promise. He left the army on the occasion of his marriage with a very beautiful girl, the daughter of a Leicestershire baronet; and I partially lost sight of him for some little time afterwards. I can, however, vouch for the accuracy of the principal facts herein narrated, and of the story generally; the sad fate of the family having made a profound impression, not only in the district in Ireland where the tragedy occurred, but throughout the country.

"(Signed) WILLIAM J. PORLOCK,
"Lieut.-Col., ——Regt.
"The Curragh, Co. Kildare."

At last she is dead!

It came to an end today: all that long agony, those heart-rending cries and moans, the terrified shuddering of that poor,

wasted body, the fixed and maddened glare, more awful for
its very unconsciousness. Only this very day they faded out
and died one by one, as death crept at last up the tortured and
emaciated limbs, and I stood over my wife's body, and tried
to thank God for both our sakes that it was all over.

And yet it was I who had done it. I who killed her—not
meaningly or of intent (I will swear that), not even so that the
laws of this earth can punish me; but truly, wilfully all the
same; of my own brutal, thoughtless selfishness. I put it all down
in my diary at the time. I tear out the pages that refer to it
now, and insert them here, that when those few friends who still
care for me hear of the end they may know how it came about.

June 10th, 1878. Castle Kilmoyle, Kerry—Arrived here today
with K. after a hard battle to get away from Lily, who couldn't
bear me going, and tried all manner of arguments to keep me
from leaving her.

"What have *you* to do with Lord Kilmoyle's tenants?" she
would keep on asking. "They owe no rent to you. Oh, Harry,
do let them alone and stay here. If you go with him you'll be
sure to come in for some of the ill-feeling that already exists
against himself; and I shall be so miserably anxious all the
time. Pray don't go."

I told her, however, that I must; first, because I had promised, and men don't like going back from their word without
any cause; and secondly, because Kilmoyle would be desperately
offended with me if I did. The fact is, I hadn't seen him for
three years till we met at that tennis-party at the Fitz Herbert's
last week; and when he asked me if I would like to run over for
a week's fishing at his place in Ireland, and help him to enforce
the eviction of a tenant who declined either to pay for the house
he lived in or leave it, I accepted with effusion. It would be a
spree. I had nothing to do, and I really wanted a little change
and waking up. As for Lily, her condition naturally makes me
rather nervous and fanciful at present, and to have me dancing
attendance on her does her more harm than good. I told her so,
and asked her, with half a dozen kisses, if she'd like to tie me to

her apron-string altogether. She burst out crying, and said she would! There is no use in reasoning with the dear little girl at present. She is better with her sisters.

June 12th—We have begun the campaign by giving the tenant twenty-four hours' notice to quit or pay. Kilmoyle and I rode down with the bailiff to the cottage, a well-built stone one in the loveliest glen ever dreamt of out of fairyland, to see it served ourselves. The door was shut and barred, and as no answer save a fierce barking from within responded to our knocks, we were beginning to think that the tenant had saved us the trouble of evicting him by decamping of his own accord, when, on crossing round the side of the house where there was a small unglazed window, we came in full view of him, seated as coolly as possible beside a bare hearthstone, with a pipe in his mouth and a big brown dog between his knees. His hair, which was snow-white, hung over his shoulders, and his face was browned to the colour of mahogany by exposure to sun and wind; but he might have been carved out of mahogany too for all the sign of attention that he gave while the bailiff repeated his messages, until Kilmoyle, losing patience, tossed a written copy of the notice into him through the open window, with a threat that, unless he complied with it, he would be smoked out of the place like a rat; after which we rode off, followed by a perfect pandemonium of barks and howls from the dog, a lean and hideous mongrel, who seemed to be only held by force from flying at our throats.

We had a jolly canter over the hills afterwards, selected the bit of river that seemed most suitable for our fishing on the morrow; and wound up the day with a couple of bottles of champagne at dinner, after which Kilmoyle was warmed up into making me an offer which I accepted on the spot—i.e., to let me have the identical cottage we had been visiting rent free, with right of shooting and fishing, for two years, on condition only of my putting and keeping it in order for that time. I wonder what Lily will say to the idea. She hates Ireland almost as much as Kilmoyle's tenants are supposed to hate him, but really it would cost mighty little to make a most picturesque little place of the cabin in question, and I believe we should both find it highly enjoyable to run down here for a couple of months' change in the autumn, after a certain and much-looked-forward-to event is well over.

June 19th—The job is done, and the man out; and Kilmoyle and I shook hands laughingly today over our victory as he handed me the key in token of my new tenantship. It has been rather an exciting bit of work, however; for the fellow—an ill-conditioned old villain, who hasn't paid a stiver of rent for the last twelve months, and only a modicum for the three previous years—*wouldn't* quit; set all threats, persuasions, and warnings at defiance, and simply sat within his door with a loaded gun in his hand, and kept it pointed at anyone who tried to approach him. In the end, and to avoid bloodshed, we had to smoke him out. There was nothing else for it, for though we took care that none of the neighbours should come near the house with food, he was evidently prepared to starve where he was rather than budge an inch; and on the third day, Donovan, the bailiff, told Kilmoyle that if he didn't want it to come to that, he must have in the help either of the "peelers" or a bit of smoke.

Kilmoyle vowed he wouldn't have the peelers anyhow. He had said he'd put the man out himself, and he'd do it; and the end of it was, we first had the windows shuttered up from outside, a sod put in the chimney, and then the door taken off its hinges while the tenant's attention was momentarily distracted by the former operations. Next, a good big fire of damp weeds which had been piled up outside was set alight, and after that there was nothing to do but wait.

It didn't take long. The wind was blowing strongly in the direction of the house, and the dense volume of thick, acrid smoke would have driven me out in about five minutes. As for the tenant, he was probably more hardened on the subject of atmosphere generally, for he managed to stand it for nearly half an hour, and until Kilmoyle and I were almost afraid to keep it up lest he should let himself be smothered out of sheer obstinacy. Just as I was debating, however, whether I wouldn't brave his gun, and make a rush for him at all costs, nature or vindictiveness got the better of his perversity; a dark figure staggered through the stifling vapour to the door, fired wildly in the direction of Kilmoyle (without hitting him, thank God!), and then dropped, a miserable object, purple with suffocation and black with smoke, upon the threshold, whence some of the keepers dragged him out into the fresh air and poured a glass of whisky down his throat, just too late to prevent his fainting away.

Five minutes later the fire was out, the windows opened, and two stalwart Scotch keepers put in charge of the dwelling, while Kilmoyle and I went home to dinner, and the wretched old man, who had given us so much trouble for nothing, was conveyed in a handcart to the village by some of his neighbours, who had been looking on from a distance, and beguiling the time by hooting and groaning at us.

"Who wants the police in these cases?" said Kilmoyle triumphantly. "To my mind, Glennie, it's mere cowardice to send for those poor fellows to enforce orders we ought to be able to carry out for ourselves, and so get them into odium with the whole neighbourhood. We managed this capitally by ourselves—and, upon my word, I couldn't help agreeing heartily with him. Indeed, the whole affair had gone off with only one trifling accident, and that was no one's fault but the tenant's.

It seems that for the last two days his abominable dog had been tied up in a miserable little pigsty a few yards from the house, Donovan having threatened him that if the brute flew at or bit anyone it would be shot instantly. Nobody was aware of this, however, and unfortunately, when the bonfire was at its height, a blazing twig fell on the roof of this little shelter and set it alight; the clouds of smoke which were blowing that way hiding what had happened until the wretched animal inside was past rescue; while even its howls attracted no attention, from the simple fact that not only it, but a score of other curs belonging to the neighbours round had been making as much noise as they could from the commencement of the affair.

Now, of course, we hear that the evicted tenant goes about swearing that we deliberately and out of malice burnt his only friend alive, and calling down curses on our heads in consequence. I don't think we are much affected by them, however. Why didn't he untie the poor brute himself? ...

June 22nd—A letter from Lady Fitz Herbert, Lily's eldest sister, telling me she thinks I had better come back at once! L. not at all well, nervous about me, and made more, instead of less so, by my account of our successful raid. What a fool I was to write it! I thought she would be amused; but the only thing now is to get back as quickly as possible, and I started this morning, Kilmoyle driving me to the station. We were bowling along pretty fast, when, as we turned a bend in the road, the horse swerved suddenly to one side, and the off-wheel of the trap went over something with that sickening sort of jolt, the meaning of which some of us know, by experience, and which made Kilmoyle exclaim:

"Good heavens, we've run over something!"

Fortunately nothing to hurt! Nothing but the carcase of a dead dog, whose charred and blackened condition would have sufficiently identified it with the victim of Tuesday's bonfire, even if we had not now perceived its late owner seated among the heather near the roadside, and occupied in pouring forth a string of wailing sounds, which might have been either prayers or curses for aught we could tell; the while he waved his shaggy white head and brown claw-like hands to and fro in unison. I yelled at him to know why he had left his brute of a dog there to upset travellers, but he paid no attention, and did not seem to hear, and as we were in a hurry to catch the train we could not afford to waste words on him, but drove on.

June 26th. Holly Lodge, West Kensington—This day sees me the proud father of a son and heir, now just five hours old, and, though rather too red for beauty, a very sturdy youngster, with a fine pair of lungs of his own. Lily says she is too happy to live, and as the dread of losing her has been the one thought of the last twenty-four hours, it is a comfort to know from the doctor that this means she has got through it capitally, and is doing as well as can be expected. Thank God for all His mercies!

July 17th—Lily has had a nasty fright this evening, for which I hope she won't be any the worse. She was lying on a couch out in the veranda for the first time since her convalescence, and I had been reading to her till she fell asleep, when I closed the book, and leaving the bell beside her in case she should want anything, went into my study to write letters. I hadn't been there for half an hour, however, when I was startled by a cry from Lily's voice and a sharp ringing of the bell, which made me fling open the study window and dart round to the veranda at the back of the house. It was empty, but in the drawing-room within, Lily was standing upright, trembling with terror and clinging to her maid, while she tried to explain to her that there was *someone* hidden in the veranda or close by, though so incoherently, owing to the state of agitation she was in, that it was not until I and the man-servant had searched veranda, garden, and outbuildings, and found nothing, that I was even able to understand what had frightened her.

It appeared then that she had suddenly been awakened from sleep by the pressure of a heavy hand on her shoulder, and a hot breath—so close, it seemed as if someone were about to whisper in her ear—upon her cheek. She started up, crying out, "Who's that? What is it?" but was only answered by a hasty withdrawal of the pressure, and the pit-pat of heavy but shoeless feet retreating through the dusk to the further end of the veranda. In a sudden access of ungovernable terror she screamed out, sprang to her feet, ringing the bell as she did so, and rushed into the drawing-room, where she was fortunately joined by her maid, who had been passing through the hall when the bell rang.

Well, as I said, we searched high and low, and not a trace of any intruder could we find; nay, not even a stray cat or dog, and we have none of our own. The garden isn't large, and there is neither tree nor shrub in it big enough to conceal a boy. The gate leading into the road was fastened inside, and the wall is too high for easy climbing; while the maid having been in the hall, could certify that no one had passed out through the drawing-room. Finally I came to the conclusion that the whole affair was the outcome of one of those very vivid dreams which some-times come to us in the semi-conscious moment between sleep and waking; and though Lily, of course, wouldn't hear of such an idea, for a long while, I think even she began to give into it after the doctor had been sent for, and had pronounced it the only rational one, and given her a composing draught before sending her off to bed. At present she is sleeping soundly, but it has been a disturbing evening, and I'm glad it's over.

September 20th—Have seen Dr C— today, and he agrees with me—that there is nothing for it but change and bracing air. He declares that the fright Lily had in July must have been much more serious than we imagined, and that she has never got over it. She *seemed* to do so. She was out and about after her confinement as soon as other people; but I remember now her nerves seemed gone from the first. She was always starting, listening, and trembling without any cause, except that she appeared in constant alarm lest something should happen to the baby; and as I took that to be a common weakness with young mothers over their first child, I'm afraid I paid no attention to it. We've a very nice nurse for the boy, a young Irish-woman named Bridget McBean (not that she's ever seen Ireland herself, but her parents came from there, driven by poverty to earn their living elsewhere, and after faithfully sending over every farthing they could screw out of their own necessities to "the ould folks at home", died in the same poverty here). Bridget is devoted to the child, and as long as he is in her care Lily generally seems easy and peaceful. Otherwise (and some strange instinct seems to tell her when this is the case) she gets nervous at once, and is always restless and uneasy.

Once she awoke with a scream in the middle of the night, declaring, "Something was wrong with the baby. Nurse had gone away and left it; she was sure of it!" To pacify her I threw on my dressing-gown and ran up to the nursery to see; and, true enough, though the boy was all right and sound asleep, Nurse was absent, having gone up to the cook's room to get something for her toothache. She came back the next moment, and I returned to satisfy Lily, but she would scarcely listen to me.

"Is it *gone?*" she asked. "Was the nursery door open? Oh, if it had been! Thank God, you were in time to drive the thing down. But how—how could it have got into the house?"

"*It?* What?" I repeated, staring.

"The dog you passed on the stairs. I saw it as it ran past the door—*a big black dog!*"

"My dear, you're dreaming. I passed no dog; nothing at all."

"Oh, Harry, didn't you see it then? I did, though it went by so quietly. Oh, is it in the house still?"

I seized the candle, went up and down stairs and searched the whole house thoroughly; but again found nothing. The fancied dog must have been a shadow on the wall only, and I told her so pretty sharply; yet on two subsequent occasions when, for some reason or another, she had the child's cot put beside her own bed at night, I was woke by finding her sitting up and shaking with fright, while she assured me that some-thing—*some animal*—had been trying to get into the room. She could hear its breathing distinctly as it scratched at the door to open it! Dr C— is right. Her nerves are clearly all wrong, and a thorough change is the only thing for her. How glad I am that the builder writes me my Kerry shooting-box is finished! We'll run over there next week . . .

September 26th, The Cabin, Kilmoyle Castle, Kerry— Certainly this place is Paradise after London, and never did I imagine that by rasing the roof so as to transform a garret into a large, bright attic, quite big enough for a nursery, throwing out a couple of bay windows into the two rooms below, and turning an adjoining barn into a kitchen and servants' room, this cottage could ever have been made into such a jolly little box. As for Lily, she's delighted with it, and looks ever so much better already. Am getting my guns in order for tomorrow, anticipating a pleasant day's shooting.

September 27th—Here's an awful bother! Bridget has given warning and declares she will leave today! It seems she knew her mother came from Kerry, and this morning she has found out that the old man who lived in this very cottage was her own grandfather, and that he died of a broken heart within a week of his eviction, having first called down a solemn curse on Kilmoyle and me, and all belonging to us, in this world and the next. They also say that he managed to scoop out a grave for his dog, and bury it right in front of the cabin door; and now Bridget is alternately tearing her hair for ever having served under her "grandfather's murtherer", and weeping over the murderer's baby the while she packs her box for departure. That wouldn't matter so much, though it's awfully unpleasant; for the housekeeper at the Castle will send us someone to mind the boy till we get another nurse; but the disclosure seems to have driven Lily as frantic as Bridget. She entreated me with tears and sobs to give up the cabin, and take her and baby back to England before "the curse could fall upon us", and wept like one brokenhearted when I told her she must be mad even to suggest such a thing after all the expense I had been to. All the same, it's a horrid nuisance. She has been crying all day, and if this fancy grows on her the change will do her no good, and I shan't know what to do. I'm sorry I was cross to her, poor child, but I was rather out of sorts myself, having been kept awake all night by the ceaseless mournful howling of some unseen cur. Besides, I'm bothered about Kilmoyle. He arranged long ago to be here this week; but the bailiff says he has been ill and is travelling, and speaks in a mysterious way as if the illness were D.T. I hope not! I had no idea before that my old chum was even addicted to drink. Anyhow, I won't be baulked of a few days shooting, at all events, and perhaps by that time Lily will have calmed down.

October 19th, The Castle—It is weeks since I opened this, and I only do so now before closing it for ever. I shall never dare to look at it again after writing down what I must today. I did go out for my shooting on the morning after my last entry, and my wife, with the babe in her arms, stood at the cabin door to see me off. The sunlight shone full on them—on the tear-stains still dark under her sweet blue eyes, and the downy head and tiny face of the infant on her breast. But she smiled as I kissed my hand to her. I shall never forget that—the last smile that *ever* ... The woman we had brought with us as servant told me the rest. She said her mistress went on playing with the child in the sunshine till it fell asleep and then laid it in its cot inside, and sat beside it rocking it. By-and-by, however, the maid went in and asked her to come and look at something that was wrong with the new kitchen arrangements, and Lily came out with her. They were in the kitchen about ten minutes, when they heard a wail from the cabin, and both ran out. Lily was first, and cried out:

"Oh, Heaven! Look! what's *that*—that great dog, *all black and burnt-looking*, coming out of the house? Oh, my baby! My baby!"

The maid saw no dog, and stopped for an instant to look round for it, letting her mistress run on. Then she heard one wild shriek from within—such a shriek as she had never heard in all her life before—and followed. She found Lily lying senseless on the floor, and in the cradle the child—stone dead! Its throat had been torn open by some savage animal, and on the bedclothes and the fresh white matting covering the floor were the blood-stained imprints of a dog's feet!

That was three weeks ago. It was evening when I came back; came back to hear my wife's delirious shrieks piercing the autumn twilight—those shrieks which, from the moment of her being roused from the merciful insensibility which held her for the first hours of her loss, she has never ceased to utter. We have moved her to the Castle since then; but I can hear them now. She has never regained consciousness once. The doctors fear she never will.

And she never did! That last entry in my diary was written two years ago. For two years my young wife, the pretty girl who loved me so dearly, and whom I took from such a happy home, has been a raving lunatic—obliged to be guarded, held down, and confined behind high walls. They have been my own walls, and I have been her keeper. The doctors wanted me to send her to an asylum; said it would be for her good, and on that I consented; but she grew so much worse there, her frantic struggles and shrieks for me to come to her, to "save her from the dog, to keep it off", were so incessant and heart-rending that they sent for me; and I have never left her again. God only knows what that means; what the horror and agony of those two years, those ceaseless, piteous cries for her child, *our* child, those agonized entreaties to me "not to go with Kilmoyle; to take her away, away"; those—oh! how have I ever borne it! . . .

Today it is over. She is dead; and—I scarce dare leave her even yet! Never once in all this time have I been tempted to share the horrible delusion which, beginning in a weak state of health, and confirmed by the awful coincidence of our baby's death, upset my darling's brain; and yet now—now that it is over, I feel as if the madness which slew her were coming on me also. As she lay dying last night, and I watched by her alone, I seemed to hear a sound of snuffling and scratching at the door outside, as though some animal were there. Once, indeed, I strode to it and threw it open, but there was nothing—nothing but a dark, fleeting shadow seen for one moment, and the sound of soft, unshod feet going pit, pat, pit, pat, upon the stairs as they retreated downwards. It was but fancy; my own heart-beats, as I knew; and yet—yet if the women who turned me out an hour ago should have left her alone—if that sound *now*—

Here the writing came to an abrupt end, the pen lying in a blot across it. At the inquest held subsequently the footman deposed that he heard his master fling open the study door, and rush violently upstairs to the death-chamber above. A loud exclamation, and the report of a pistol-shot followed almost immediately; and on running to the rescue he found Captain Glennie standing inside the door, his face livid with horror, and the revolver in his outstretched hand still pointed at a corner of the room on the other side of the bier, the white covering on which had in one place been dragged off and torn. Before the man could speak, however, his master turned round to him, and exclaiming:

"Williams, *I have seen it*! It was there! *On her*! Better this than a madhouse! There is no other escape," put the revolver to his head, and fired. He was dead ere even the servant could catch him.

LOUIS

by Saki

SAKI WAS THE nom de guerre *chosen by the Scottish humorist Hector Hugh Munro (1870–1916) with which to sign his enjoyably malicious satires. Undoubtedly one of the most talented entertaining writers of his generation, he died in action during the Great War.*

In Beware of the Cat *Saki introduced us to that outrageously extrovert cat, Tobermory. His canine counterpart, Louis, may not be quite as demonstrative as Tobermory but in his own quiet way he is just as outrageous . . .*

"It would be jolly to spend Easter in Vienna this year," said Strudwarden, "and look up some of my old friends there. It's about the jolliest place I know of to be at for Easter—"

"I thought we had made up our minds to spend Easter at Brighton," interrupted Lena Strudwarden, with an air of aggrieved surprise.

"You mean that you had made up your mind that we should spend Easter there," said her husband; "we spent last Easter there, and Whitsuntide as well, and the year before that we were at Worthing, and Brighton again before that. I think it would be just as well to have a real change of scene while we are about it."

"The journey to Vienna would be very expensive," said Lena.

"You are not often concerned about economy," said Strudwarden, "and in any case the trip to Vienna won't cost a bit more than the rather meaningless luncheon parties we usually give to quite meaningless acquaintances at Brighton. To escape from all that set would be a holiday in itself."

Strudwarden spoke feelingly; Lena Strudwarden maintained an equally feeling silence on that particular subject. The set that she gathered round her at Brighton and other South Coast resorts was composed of individuals who might be dull and meaningless in themselves, but who understood the art of flattering Mrs Strudwarden. She had no intention of forgoing their society and their homage and flinging herself among unappreciative strangers in a foreign capital.

"You must go to Vienna alone if you are bent on going," she said; "I couldn't leave Louis behind, and a dog is always a fearful nuisance in a foreign hotel, besides all the fuss and separation of the quarantine restrictions when one comes back. Louis would die if he was parted from me for even a week. You don't know what that would mean to me."

Lena stooped down and kissed the nose of the diminutive brown Pomeranian that lay, snug and irresponsive, beneath a shawl on her lap.

"Look here," said Strudwarden, "this eternal Louis business is getting to be a ridiculous nuisance. Nothing can be done, no plans can be made, without some veto connected with that animal's whims or convenience being imposed. If you were a priest in attendance on some African fetish you couldn't set up a more elaborate code of restrictions. I believe you'd ask the Government to put off a General Election if you thought it would interfere with Louis's comfort in any way."

By way of answer to this tirade Mrs Strudwarden stooped down again and kissed the irresponsive brown nose. It was the action of a woman with a beautifully meek nature, who would, however, send the whole world to the stake sooner than yield an inch where she knew herself to be in the right.

"It isn't as if you were in the least bit fond of animals," went on Strudwarden, with growing irritation; "when we are down at Kerryfield you won't stir a step to take the house dogs out, even if they're dying for a run, and I don't think you've been in the stables twice in your life. You laugh at what you call the fuss that's being made over the extermination of plumage birds, and you are quite indignant with me if I interfere on behalf of an ill-treated, over-driven animal on the road. And yet you insist on everyone's plans being made subservient to the convenience of that stupid little morsel of fur and selfishness."

"You are prejudiced against my little Louis," said Lena, with a world of tender regret in her voice.

"I've never had the chance of being anything else but prejudiced against him," said Strudwarden; "I know what a jolly responsive companion a doggie can be, but I've never been allowed to put a finger near Louis. You say he snaps at any one except you and your maid, and you snatched him away from old Lady Peterby the other day, when she wanted to pet him, for fear he would bury his teeth in her. All that I ever see of him is the tip of his unhealthy-looking little nose, peeping out from his basket or from your muff, and I occasionally hear his wheezy little bark when you take him for a walk up and down the corridor. You can't expect one to get extravagantly fond of a dog of that sort. One might as well work up an affection for the cuckoo in a cuckoo-clock."

"He loves me," said Lena, rising from the table, and bearing the shawl-swathed Louis in her arms. "He loves only me, and perhaps that is why I love him so much in return. I don't care what you say against him, I am not going to be separated from him. If you insist on going to Vienna you must go alone, as far as I am concerned. I think it would be much more sensible if you were to come to Brighton with Louis and me, but of course you must please yourself."

"You must get rid of that dog," said Strudwarden's sister when Lena had left the room; "it must be helped to some sudden and merciful end. Lena is merely making use of it as an instrument for getting her own way on dozens of occasions when she would otherwise be obliged to yield gracefully to your wishes or to the general convenience. I am convinced that she doesn't care a brass button about the animal itself. When her friends are buzzing round her at Brighton or anywhere else and the dog would be in the way, it has to spend whole days alone with the maid, but if you want Lena to go with you anywhere where she doesn't want to go instantly she trots out the excuse that she couldn't be separated from her dog. Have you ever come into a room unobserved and heard Lena talking to her beloved pet? I never have. I believe she only fusses over it when there's someone present to notice her."

"I don't mind admitting," said Strudwarden, "that I've dwelt more than once lately on the possibility of some fatal accident putting an end to Louis's existence. It's not very easy, though, to arrange a fatality for a creature that spends most of its time in a muff or asleep in a toy kennel. I don't think poison would be any good; it's obviously horribly over-fed, for I've seen Lena offer it dainties at table sometimes, but it never seems to eat them."

"Lena will be away at church on Wednesday morning," said Elsie Strudwarden reflectively; "she can't take Louis with her there, and she is going on to the Dellings for lunch. That will give you several hours in which to carry out your purpose. The maid will be flirting with the chauffeur most of the time, and, anyhow, I can manage to keep her out of the way on some pretext or other."

"That leaves the field clear," said Strudwarden, "but unfortunately my brain is equally a blank as far as any lethal project is concerned. The little beast is so monstrously inactive; I can't pretend that it leapt into the bath and drowned itself, or that it took on the butcher's mastiff in unequal combat and got chewed up. In what possible guise could death come to a confirmed basket-dweller? It would be too suspicious if we invented a Suffragette raid and pretended that they invaded Lena's boudoir and threw a brick at him. We should have to do a lot of other damage as well, which would be rather a nuisance, and the servants would think it odd that they had seen nothing of the invaders."

"I have an idea," said Elsie; "get a box with an air-tight lid, and bore a small hole in it, just big enough to let in an india-rubber tube. Pop Louis, kennel and all, into the box, shut it down, and put the other end of the tube under the gas-bracket. There you have a perfect lethal chamber. You can stand the kennel at the open window afterwards, to get rid of the smell of the gas, and all that Lena will find when she comes home late in the afternoon will be a placidly defunct Louis."

"Novels have been written about women like you," said Strudwarden; "you have a perfectly criminal mind. Let's come and look for a box."

Two minutes later the conspirators stood gazing guiltily at a stout square box, connected with the gas-bracket by a length of india-rubber tubing.

"Not a sound," said Elsie; "he never stirred; it must have been quite painless. All the same I feel rather horrid now it's done."

"The ghastly part has to come," said Strudwarden, turning off the gas. "We'll lift the lid slowly, and let the gas out by degrees. Swing the door to and fro to send a draught through the room."

Some minutes later, when the fumes had rushed off, he stooped down and lifted out the little kennel with its grim burden. Elsie gave an exclamation of terror. Louis sat at the door of his dwelling, head erect and ears pricked, as coldly and defiantly inert as when they had put him into his execution chamber. Strudwarden dropped the kennel with a jerk, and stared for a long moment at the miracle-dog; then he went into a peal of chattering laughter.

It was certainly a wonderful imitation of a truculent-looking toy Pomeranian, and the apparatus that gave forth a wheezy bark when you pressed it had materially helped the imposition that Lena, and Lena's maid, had foisted on the household. For a woman who disliked animals, but liked getting her own way under a halo of unselfishness, Mrs. Strudwarden had managed rather well.

"Louis is dead," was the curt information that greeted Lena on her return from her luncheon party.

"Louis *dead*!" she exclaimed.

"Yes, he flew at the butcher-boy and bit him, and he bit me too, when I tried to get him off, so I had to have him destroyed. You warned me that he snapped, but you didn't tell me that he was downright dangerous. I shall have to pay the boy something heavy by way of compensation, so you will have to go without those buckles that you wanted to have for Easter; also I shall have to go to Vienna to consult Dr Schroeder, who is a specialist on dogbites, and you will have to come too. I have sent what remains of Louis to Rowland Ward to be stuffed; that will be my Easter gift to you instead of the buckles. For Heaven's sake, Lena, weep, if you really feel it so much; anything would be better than standing there staring as if you thought I had lost my reason."

Lena Strudwarden did not weep, but her attempt at laughing was an unmistakable failure.

by Fritz Leiber

FOR OVER THIRTY *years, Fritz Leiber has been a leading American master of Fantasy and Science Fiction, successfully weathering all changes in literary fashion and public taste. Five times he has won the coveted Hugo Award for the best SF story of the year and his characteristically stylish stories have been adapted for both big and small screen. Recently he has been teaching creative writing in a San Francisco college.*

The Howling Tower, one of Mr Leiber's earliest published stories, is part of a deliciously-characterized series of tales about giant Fafhrd and his diminutive companion, the Grey Mouser, two Rogues of Fortune seeking adventures in the ancient, magical land of Nehwon.

The sound was not loud, yet it seemed to fill the whole vast, darkening plain, and the palely luminous, hollow sky: a wailing and howling, so faint and monotonous that it might have been inaudible save for the pulsing rise and fall; an ancient, ominous sound that was somehow in harmony with the wild, sparsely vegetated landscape and the barbaric garb of the three men who sheltered in a little dip in the ground, lying close to a dying fire.

"Wolves, perhaps," Fafhrd said. "I have heard them howl that way on the Cold Waste when they hunted me down. But a whole ocean sunders us from the Cold Waste and there's a difference between the sounds, Grey Mouser."

The Mouser pulled his grey woollen cloak closer around him. Then he and Fafhrd looked at the third man, who had not spoken. The third man was meanly clad, and his cloak was ragged and the scabbard of his short sword was frayed. With surprise, they saw that his eyes stared, white circled, from his pinched, leathery face and that he trembled.

"You've been over these plains many times before," Fafhrd said to him, speaking the guttural language of the guide. "That's why we've asked you to show us the way. You must know this country well." The last words pointed the question.

The guide gulped, nodded jerkily. "I've heard it before, not so loud," he said in a quick, vague voice. "Not at this time of year. Men have been known to vanish. There are stories. They say men hear it in their dreams and are lured away—not a good sound."

"No wolf's a good wolf," rumbled Fafhrd amusedly.

It was still light enough for the Mouser to catch the obstinate, guarded look on the guide's face as he went on talking.

"I never saw a wolf in these parts, nor spoke with a man who killed one." He paused, then rambled off abstractedly. "They tell of an old tower somewhere out on the plains. They say the sound is strongest there. I have not seen it. They say—"

Abruptly he stopped. He was not trembling now, seemed withdrawn into himself. The Mouser prodded him with a few tempting questions, but the answers were little more than mouth noises, neither affirmative nor negative.

The fire glowed through white ashes, died. A little wind rustled the scant grasses. The sound had ceased now, or else it had sunk so deeply into their minds that it was no longer audible. The Mouser, peering sleepily over the humped horizon of Fafhrd's great cloaked body, turned his thoughts to far-off, many-taverned Lankhmar, leagues and leagues away across alien lands and a whole uncharted ocean. The limitless darkness pressed down.

Next morning the guide was gone. Fafhrd laughed and made light of the occurrence as he stood stretching and snuffing the cool, clear air.

"Foh! I could tell these plains were not to his liking, for all his talk of having crossed them seven times. A bundle of superstitious fears! You saw how he quaked when the little wolves began to howl. My word on it, he's run back to his friends we left at the last water."

The Mouser, fruitlessly scanning the empty horizon, nodded without conviction. He felt through his pouch.

"Well, at least he's not robbed us—except for the two gold pieces we gave him to bind the bargain."

Fafhrd's laughter pealed and he thumped the Mouser between the shoulder blades. The Mouser caught him by the wrist, threw him with a twist and a roll, and they wrestled on the ground until the Mouser was pinned.

"Come on," grinned Fafhrd, springing up. "It won't be the first time we've travelled strange country alone."

They tramped far that day. The springiness of the Mouser's wiry body enabled him to keep up with Fafhrd's long strides. Towards evening a whirring arrow from Fafhrd's bow brought down a sort of small antelope with delicately ridged horns. A little earlier they had found an unsullied waterhole and filled their skin bags. When the late summer sunset came, they made camp and munched carefully broiled loin and crisped bits of fat.

The Mouser sucked his lips and fingers clean, then strolled to the top of a nearby hummock to survey the line of their next day's march. The haze that had curtailed vision during the afternoon was gone now, and he could peer far over the rolling, swelling grasslands through the cool, tangy air. At that moment the road to Lankhmar did not seem so long, or so weary. Then his sharp eyes spied an irregularity in the horizon towards which they were tending. Too distinct for trees, too evenly shaped for rocks; and he had seen no trees or rock in this country. It stood out sharp and tiny against the pale sky. No, it was built by man; a tower of some sort.

At that moment the sound returned. It seemed to come from everywhere at once; as if the sky itself were wailing faintly, as if the wide, solid ground were baying mournfully. It was louder this time, and there was in it a strange confusion of sadness and threat, grief and menace.

Fafhrd jumped to his feet and waved his arms strongly, and the Mouser heard him bellow out in a great, jovial voice, "Come, little wolves, come and share our fire and singe your cold noses. I will send my bronze-beaked birds winging to welcome you, and my friend will show you how a slung stone can buzz like a bee. We will teach you the mysteries of sword and axe. Come, little wolves, and be guests of Fafhrd and the Grey Mouser! Come, little wolves—or biggest of them all!"

The huge laugh with which he ended this challenge drowned out the alien sound and it seemed slow in reasserting itself, as though laughter were a stronger thing. The Mouser felt cheered and it was with a light heart that he told Fafhrd of what he had seen, and reminded him of what the guide had said about the noise and the tower.

Fafhrd only laughed again and guessed, "Perhaps the sad, furry ones have a den there. We shall find out tomorrow, since we go that way. I would like to kill a wolf."

The big man was in a jolly mood and would not talk with the Mouser about serious or melancholy things. Instead, he sang drinking songs and repeated old tavern jokes, chuckling hugely and claiming that they made him feel as drunk as wine. He kept up such an incessant clamour that the Mouser could not tell whether the strange howling had ceased, though he rather imagined he heard it once or twice. Certainly it was gone by the time they wrapped themselves up for sleep in the wraithlike starlight.

Next morning Fafhrd was gone. Even before the Mouser had halooed for him and scanned the nearby terrain, he knew that his foolish, self-ridiculed fears had become certainties. He could still see the tower, although in the flat, yellow light of morning it seemed to have receded, as though it were seeking to evade him. He even fancied he saw a tiny moving figure nearer to the tower than to him. That, he knew, was only imagination. The distance was too great. Nevertheless, he wasted little time in chewing and swallowing some cold meat, which still had a savoury taste, in wrapping up some more for his pouch, and in taking a gulp of water. Then he set out at a long, springy lope, a pace he knew he could hold for hours.

At the bottom of the next swell in the plain he found slightly softer ground, cast up and down it for Fafhrd's footprints and found them. They were wide-spaced, made by a man running.

Towards midday he found a waterhole, lay down to drink and rest a little. A short way back he had again seen Fafhrd's prints. Now he noted another set in the soft earth; not Fafhrd's, but roughly parallel to his. They were at least a day older, wide-spaced, too, but a little wobbly. From their size and shape they might very well have been made by the guide's sandals; the middle of the print showed faintly the mark of thongs such as he had worn about the instep.

The Mouser loped doggedly on. His pouch, rolled cloak, water bag, and weapons were beginning to feel a burden. The tower was appreciably closer, although the sun haze masked any details. He calculated he had covered almost half the distance.

The slight successive swells in the prairieland seemed as endless as those in a dream. He noticed them not so much by sight as by the infinitesimal hindrance and easing they gave his lope. The little low clumps of bush and brush by which he measured his progress were all the same. The infrequent gullies were no wider than could be taken in a stride. Once a coiled greenish serpent raised its flat head from the rock on which it was sunning and observed his passing. Occasionally grasshoppers whirred out of his path. He ran with his feet close to the ground to conserve energy, yet there was a strong, forward leap to his stride, for he was used to matching that of a taller man. His nostrils flared wide, sucking and expelling air. The wide mouth was set. There was a grim, fixed look to the black eyes above the browned cheeks. He knew that even at his best he would be hard put to equal the speed in Fafhrd's rangy, long-muscled frame.

Clouds sailed in from the north, casting great, hurrying shadows over the landscape, finally blotting out the sun altogether. He could see the tower better now. It was of a dark colour, with black specks that might be small windows.

It was while he was pausing atop a rise for a breathing spell that the sound recommenced, taking him unawares, sending a shiver over his flesh. It might have been the low clouds that gave it greater power and an eerie, echoing quality. It might have been his being alone that made it seem less sorrowful and more menacing. But it was undeniably louder, and its rhythmic swells came like great gusts of wind.

The Mouser had counted on reaching the tower by sunset. But the early appearance of the sound upset his calculations and did not bode well for Fafhrd. His judgment told him he could cover the rest of the distance at something like top speed. Instantly he came to a decision. He tossed his big pouch, waterskin, bundled cloak, sword, and harness into a clump of bushes; kept only his light inner jerkin, long dagger, and sling. Thus lightened, he spurted ahead, feet flying. The low clouds darkened. A few drops of rain spattered. He kept his eyes on the ground, watching for inequalities and slippery spots. The sound seemed to intensify and gain new unearthliness of timbre with every bounding stride he took forward.

Away from the tower the plain had been empty and vast, but here it was desolate. The sagging or tumbled wooden outbuildings, the domestic grains and herbs run wild and dying out, the lines of stunted and toppled trees, the suggestion of fences and paths and ruts—all combined to give the impression that human life had once been here but had long since departed. Only the great stone tower, with its obstinate solidity, and with sound pouring from it or seeming to pour from it, was alive.

The Mouser, pretty well winded though not shaky, now changed his course and ran in an oblique direction to take advantage of the cover provided by a thin line of trees and wind-blown scrub. Such caution was second nature with him. All his instincts clamoured against the possibility of meeting a wolf or hound pack on open ground.

He had worked his way past and part way around the tower before he came to the conclusion that there was no line of concealment leading all the way up to the base. It stood a little aloof from the ruins around it.

The Mouser paused in the shelter afforded by a

weather-silvered, buckled outbuilding; automatically searched about until he found a couple of small stones whose weight suited his sling. His sturdy chest still worked like a bellows, drinking air. Then he peered around a corner at the tower and stood there crouched a little, frowning.

It was not as high as he had thought; five stories or perhaps six. The narrow windows were irregularly placed, and did not give any clear idea of inner configuration. The stones were large and rudely hewn; seemed firmly set, save for those of the battlement, which had shifted somewhat. Almost facing him was the dark, uninformative rectangle of a doorway.

There was no rushing such a place, was the Mouser's thought; no sense in rushing a place that had no sign of defenders. There was no way of getting at it unseen; a watcher on the battlements would have noted his approach long ago. One could only walk up to it, tensely alert for unexpected attacks. And so the Mouser did that.

Before he had covered half the distance his sinews were taut and straining. He was mortally certain that he was being watched by something more than unfriendly. A day's running had made him a little light-headed, and his senses were abnormally clear. Against the unending hypnotic background of the howling he heard the splatters of the separate raindrops, not yet become a shower. He noted the size and shape of each dark stone around the darker doorway. He smelled the characteristic odour of stone, wood, soil, but yet no heavy animal smell. For the thousandth time he tried to picture some possible source for the sound. A dozen hound packs in a cavern underground? That was close, but not close enough. Something eluded him. And now the dark walls were very near, and he strained his eyes to penetrate the gloom of the doorway.

The remote grating sound might not have been enough of a warning, for he was almost in a trance. It may have been the sudden, very slight increase of darkness over his head that twanged the taut bowstrings of his muscles and sent him lunging with cat-like rapidity into the tower—instinctively, without pausing to glance up. Certainly he had not an instant to spare, for he felt an unyielding surface graze his escaping body and flick his heels. A spurt of wind rushed past him from behind, and the jar of a mighty impact staggered him. He spun around to see a great square of stone half obscuring the doorway. A few moments before it had formed part of the battlement.

Looking at it as it lay there denting the ground, he grinned for the first time that day and almost laughed in relief.

The silence was profound, startling. It occurred to the Mouser that the howling had ceased utterly. He glanced around the barren, circular interior, then started up the curving stone stair that hugged the wall. His grin was dangerous now, businesslike. On the first level above he found Fafhrd and—after a fashion—the guide. But he found a puzzle, too.

Like that below, the room occupied the full circumference of the tower. Light from the scattered, slit-like windows dimly revealed the chests lining the walls and the dried herbs and desiccated birds, small mammals, and reptiles hanging from the ceiling, suggesting an apothecary's shop. There was litter everywhere, but it was a tidy litter, seeming to have a tortuously logical arrangement all of its own. On a table was a hodgepodge of stoppered bottles and jars, mortars, and pestles, odd instruments of horn, glass, and bone, and a brazier in which charcoal smouldered. There was also a plate of gnawed bones and beside it a brass-bound book of parchment, spread open by a dagger set across the pages.

Fafhrd lay face-up on a bed of skins laced to a low wooden framework. He was pale and breathing heavily, looked as if he had been drugged. He did not respond when the Mouser shook him gently and whispered his name, then shook him hard and shouted it. But the thing that baffled the Mouser was the multitude of linen bandages wound around Fafhrd's limbs and chest and throat, for they were unstained and, when he parted them, there were no wounds beneath. They were obviously not bonds.

And lying beside Fafhrd, so close that his big hand touched the hilt, was Fafhrd's great sword, unsheathed.

It was only then that the Mouser saw the guide, huddled in a dark corner behind the couch. He was similarly bandaged.

But the bandages were stiff with rusty stains, and it was easy to see that he was dead.

The Mouser tried again to wake Fafhrd, but the big man's face stayed a marble mask. The Mouser did not feel that Fafhrd was actually there, and the feeling frightened and angered him.

As he stood nervously puzzling he became aware of slow steps descending the stone stair. Slowly they circled the tower. The sound of heavy breathing was heard, coming in regular gasps. The Mouser crouched behind the tables, his eyes glued on the black hole in the ceiling through which the stair vanished.

The man who emerged was old and small and bent, dressed in garments as tattered and uncouth and musty-looking as the contents of the room. He was partly bald, with a matted tangle of grey hair around his large ears. When the Mouser sprang up and menaced him with a drawn dagger he did not attempt to flee, but went into what seemed an ecstasy of fear—trembling, babbling throaty sounds, and darting his arms about meaninglessly.

The Mouser thrust a stubby candle into the brazier, held it to the old man's face. He had never seen eyes so wide with terror—they jutted out like little white balls—nor lips so thin and unfeelingly cruel.

The first intelligible words that issued from the lips were hoarse and choked; the voice of a man who has not spoken for a long time.

"You are dead. You are dead!" he cackled at the Mouser, pointing a shaky finger. "You should not be here. I killed you. Why else have I kept the great stone cunningly balanced, so that a touch would send it over? I knew you did not come because the sound lured you. You came to hurt me and to help your friend. So I killed you. I saw the stone fall. I saw you under the stone. You could not have escaped it. You are dead."

And he tottered towards the Mouser, brushing at him as though he could dissipate the Mouser like smoke. But when his hands touched solid flesh he squealed and stumbled away.

The Mouser followed him, moving his knife suggestively.

"You are right as to why I came," he said. "Give me back my friend. Rouse him."

To his surprise, the old man did not cringe, but abruptly stood his ground. The look of terror in the unblinking eyes underwent a subtle change. The terror was still there, but there was something more. Bewilderment vanished and something else took its place. He walked past the Mouser and sat down on a stool by the table.

"I am not much afraid of you," he muttered, looking sideways. "But there are those of whom I am very much afraid. And I fear you only because you will try to hinder me from protecting myself against them or taking the measures I know I must take." He became plaintive. "You must not hinder me. You must not."

The Mouser frowned. The ghastly look of terror—and something more—that warped the old man's face seemed a permanent thing, and the strange words he spoke did not sound like lies.

"Nevertheless, you must rouse my friend."

The old man did not answer this. Instead, after one quick glance at the Mouser, he stared vacantly at the wall, shaking his head, and began to talk.

"I do not fear you. Yet I know the depths of fear. You do not. Have you lived alone with *that sound* for years on years, knowing what it meant? I have.

"Fear was born into me. It was in my mother's bones and blood. And in my father's and in my brothers'. There was too much magic and loneliness in this, our home, and in my people. When I was a child they all feared and hated me—even the slaves and the great hounds that before me slavered and growled and snapped.

"But my fears were stronger than theirs, for did they not die one by one in such a way that no suspicion fell upon me until the end? I knew it was one against many, and I took no chances. When it began, they always thought I would be the next to go!" He cackled at this. "They thought I was small and weak and foolish. But did not my brothers die as if strangled by their own hands? Did not my mother sicken and languish? Did not my father give a great cry and leap from the tower's top?

"The hounds were the last to go. They hated me most—even more than my father hated me—and the smallest of them could have torn out my throat. They were hungry because there was no one left to feed them. But I lured them into the deep cellar, pretending to flee from them; and when they were all inside I slipped out and barred the door. For many a night thereafter they bayed and howled at me, but I knew I was safe. Gradually the baying grew less and less as they killed each other, but the survivors gained new life from the bodies of the slain. They lasted a long time. Eventually there was only one single thin voice left to howl vengefully at me. Each night I went to sleep, telling myself, 'Tomorrow there will be silence.' But each morning I was awakened by the cry. Then I forced myself to take a torch and go down and peer through the wicket in the door of the cellar. But though I watched for a long time there was no movement, save that of the flickering shadows, and I saw nothing but white bones and tatters of skin. And I told myself that the sound would soon go away."

The old man's thin lips were twisted into a pitiful and miserable expression that sent a chill over the Mouser.

"But the sound lived on, and after a long while it began to grow louder again. Then I knew that my cunning had been in vain. I had killed their bodies, but not their ghosts, and soon they would gain enough power to return and slay me, as they had always intended. So I studied more carefully my father's books of magic and sought to destroy their ghosts utterly or to curse them to such far-off places that they could never reach me. For a while I seemed to be succeeding, but the scales turned and they began to get the better of me. Closer and closer they came, and sometimes I seemed to catch my father's and brothers' voices, almost lost among the howling.

"It was on a night when they must have been very close that an exhausted traveller came running to the tower. There was a strange look in his eyes, and I thanked the beneficent god who had sent him to my door, for I knew what I must do. I gave him food and drink, and in his drink I mingled a liquid that enforced sleep and sent his naked ghost winging out of his body. *They* must have captured and torn it, for presently the man bled and died. But it satisfied them somewhat, for their howling went a long way off, and it was a long time before it began to creep back. Thereafter the gods were good and always sent me a guest before the sound came too close. I learned to bandage those I drugged so that they would last longer, and their deaths would satisfy the howling ones more fully."

The old man paused then, and shook his head queerly and made a vague, reproachful, clucking noise with his tongue.

"But what troubles me now," he said, "is that they have become greedier, or perhaps they have seen through my cunning. For they are less easy to satisfy, and press at me closely and never go far away. Sometimes I wake in the night, hearing them snuffing about, and feeling their muzzles at my throat. I must have more men to fight them for me. I must. He"—pointing at the stiff body of the guide—"was nothing to them. They took no more notice of him than a dry bone. That one"—his finger wavered over to Fafhrd—"is big and strong. He should hold them back for a long time."

It was dark outside now, and the only light came from the guttering candle. The Mouser glared at the old man where he sat perched on the stool like some ungainly plucked foul. Then he looked to where Fafhrd lay, watched the great chest rise and fall, saw the strong, pallid jaw jutting up over the high wrappings. And at that, a terrible anger and an unnerving boundless irritation took hold of him and he hurled himself upon the old man.

But at the instant he started his long dagger on the downward stroke the sound gushed back. It seemed to overflow from some pit of darkness, and to inundate the tower and plain so that the walls vibrated and dust puffed out from the dead things hanging from the ceiling.

The Mouser stopped the blade a hand's breadth from the throat of the old man, whose head, twisted back, jiggled in terror. For the return of the sound forcibly set the question: Could anyone but the old man save Fafhrd now? The Mouser wavered between alternatives, pushed the old man away, knelt by Fafhrd's side, shook him, spoke to him. There was no response. Then he heard the voice of the old man. It was shaky and half drowned by the sound, but it carried an almost gloating note of confidence.

"Your friend's body is poised on the brink of life. If you handle it roughly it may overbalance. If you strip off the bandages he will only die the quicker. You cannot help him." Then, reading the Mouser's question, "No, there is no antidote." Then hastily, as if he feared to take away all hope, "But he will not be defenceless against them. He is strong. His ghost may be strong, too. He may be able to weary them out. If he lives until midnight he may return."

The Mouser turned and looked up at him. Again the old man seemed to read something in the Mouser's merciless eyes, for he said, "My death by your hand will not satisfy those who howl. If you kill me, you will not save your friend, but doom him. Being cheated of my ghost, they will rend his utterly."

The wizened body trembled in an ecstasy of excitement and terror. The hands fluttered. The head bobbled back and forth, as if with the palsy. It was hard to read anything in that twitching, saucer-eyed face. The Mouser slowly got to his feet.

"Perhaps not," said the Mouser. "Perhaps as you say, your death will doom him." He spoke slowly and in a loud, measured tone. "Nevertheless, I shall take the chance of killing you right now unless you suggest something better."

"Wait," said the old man, pushing at the Mouser's dagger and drawing a pricked hand away. "Wait. There is a way you could help him. Somewhere out there"—he made a sweeping, upward gesture with his hand—"your friend's ghost is battling them. I have more of the drug left. I will give you some. Then you can fight them side by side. Together you may defeat them. But you must be quick. Look! Even now they are at him!"

The old man pointed at Fafhrd. The bandage on the barbarian's left arm was no longer unstained. There was a growing splotch of red on the left wrist—the very place where a hound might take hold. Watching it, the Mouser felt his insides grow sick and cold. The old man was pushing something into his hand. "Drink this. Drink this now," he was saying.

The Mouser looked down. It was a small glass vial. The deep purple of the liquid corresponded with the hue of a dried trickle he had seen at the corner of Fafhrd's mouth. Like a man bewitched, he plucked out the stopper, raised it slowly to his lips, paused.

"Swiftly! Swiftly!" urged the old man, almost dancing with impatience. "About half is enough to take you to your friend. The time is short. Drink! Drink!"

But the Mouser did not. Struck by a sudden, new thought, he eyed the old man over his upraised hand. And the old man must have instantly read the import of that thought, for he snatched up the dagger lying on the book and lunged at the Mouser with unexpected rapidity. Almost the thrust went home, but the Mouser recovered his wits and struck sideways with his free fist at the old man's hand so that the dagger clattered across the floor. Then, with a rapid, careful movement, the Mouser set the vial on the table. The old man darted after him, snatching at it, seeking to upset it, but the Mouser's iron grip closed on his wrists. He was forced to the floor, his arms pinioned, his head pushed back.

"Yes," said the Mouser, "I shall drink. Have no fear on that score. But you shall drink, too."

The old man gave a strangled scream and struggled convulsively. "No! No!" he cried. "Kill me! Kill me with your knife! But not the drink! Not the drink!" The Mouser, kneeling on his arms to pinion them, pried at his jaw. Suddenly he became quiet and stared up, a peculiar lucidity in his white-circled, pinpoint-pupiled eyes. "It's no use. I sought to trick you," he said. "I gave the last of the drug to your friend. The stuff you hold is poison. We shall both die miserably, and your friend will be irrevocably doomed."

But when he saw that the Mouser did not heed this, he began once more to struggle like a maniac. The Mouser was inexorable.

Although the base of his thumb was bitted deep, he forced the old man's jaws apart, held his nose and poured the thick purple liquor down. The face of the old man grew red and the veins stood out. When the gulp came it was like a death rattle. Then the Mouser drank off the rest—it was salty like blood and had a sickeningly sweet odour—and waited.

He was torn with revulsion at what he had done. Never had he inflicted such terror on man or woman before. He would much rather have killed. The look on the old man's face was grotesquely similar to that of a child under torture. Only that poor aged wretch, thought the Mouser, knew the full meaning of the howling that even now dinned menacingly in their ears. The Mouser almost let him reach the dagger towards which he was weakly squirming. But he thought of Fafhrd and gripped the old man tight.

Gradually the room filled with haze and began to swing and slowly spin. The Mouser grew dizzy. It was as if the sound were dissolving the walls. Something was wrenching at his body and prying at his mind. Then came utter blackness, whirled and shaken by a pandemonium of howling.

But there was no sound at all on the vast alien plain to which the blackness suddenly gave way. Only sight and a sense of great cold. A cloudless, sourceless moonlight revealed endless sweeps of smooth black rock and sharply edged the featureless horizon.

He was conscious of a thing that stood by him and seemed to be trying to hide behind him. Then, at a small distance, he noted a pale form which he instinctively knew to be Fafhrd. And around the pale form seethed a pack of black, shadowy animal shapes, leaping and retreating, worrying at the pale form, their eyes glowing like the moonlight, but brighter, their long muzzles soundlessly snarling. The thing beside him seemed to shrink closer. And then the Mouser rushed forward towards his friend.

The shadowy pack turned on him and he braced himself to meet their onslaught. But the leader leaped past his shoulder, and the rest divided and flowed by him like a turbulent black stream. Then he realized that the thing which had sought to hide behind him was no longer there. He turned and saw that the black shapes pursued another small pale form.

It fled fast, but they followed faster. Over sweep after sweep of rock the hunt continued. He seemed to see taller, man-shaped figures among the pack. Slowly they dwindled in size, became tiny, vague. And still the Mouser felt the horrible hate and fear that followed from them.

Then the sourceless moonlight faded, and only the cold remained, and that, too, dissipated, leaving nothing.

When he awoke, Fafhrd's face was looking down at him, and Fafhrd was saying, "Lie still, little man. Lie still. No, I'm not badly hurt. A torn hand. Not bad. No worse than your own."

But the Mouser shook his head impatiently and pushed his aching shoulder off the couch. Sunlight was knifing in through the narrow windows, revealing the dustiness of the air. Then he saw the body of the old man.

"Yes," Fafhrd said as the Mouser lay back weakly. "His fears are ended now. They've done with him. I should hate him. But who can hate such tattered flesh? When I came to the tower he gave me the drink. There was something wrong in my head. I believed what he said. He told me it would make me a god. I drank, and it sent me to a cold waste in hell. But now it's done with and we're still in Nehwon."

The Mouser, eyeing the thoroughly and unmistakably dead things that dangled from the ceiling, felt content.

THE WHITE DOG

by Feodor Sologub

FEODOR KUZ'MICH TETERNIKOV *(1863–1927), who wrote under the name of Feodor Sologub, has been described as the Russian Edgar Allan Poe. A prolific writer of short stories, novels, poetry, plays and fairy tales, Sologub belonged to the Russian Symbolist Movement, reacting against the influence of Dostoevsky and other social realists. In the west he is perhaps best known for his novel* The Petty Demon *(1902) which was inspired by his own experiences as an inspector of schools; yet his greatest work is probably* The Created Legend *(1908–1912), an ambitious and imaginative trilogy whose hero, Trivodov, is a Satanist.*

It is said that in pre-revolutionary Russia, white dogs were viewed with such superstitious dread that cab drivers would refuse to take their charges any further if one crossed their path. Around this superstition, Sologub has woven a tale of haunting ambiguity. The translation is by John Cournos.

Everything grew irksome for Alexandra Ivanovna in the work-shop of this out-of-the-way town—the pattens, the clatter of machines, the complaints of the managers; it was the shop in which she had served as apprentice and now for several years as seamstress. Everything irritated Alexandra Ivanovna; she quarrelled with everyone and abused the innocent apprentices. Among others to suffer from her outbursts of temper was Tanechka, the youngest of the seamstresses, who had only recently become an apprentice. In the beginning Tanechka submitted to her abuse in silence. In the end she revolted, and, addressing herself to her assailant, said, quite calmly and affably, so that everyone laughed:

"You, Alexandra Ivanovna, are a downright dog!"

Alexandra Ivanovna felt humiliated.

"You are a dog yourself!" she exclaimed.

Tanechka was sitting sewing. She paused now and then from her work and said in a calm, deliberate manner:

"You always whine... Certainly, you are a dog... You have a dog's snout... And a dog's ears... And a wagging tail ... The mistress will soon drive you out of doors, because you are the most detestable of dogs, a poodle."

Tanechka was a young, plump, rosy-cheeked girl with an innocent, good-natured face, which revealed, however, a trace of cunning. She sat there so demurely, barefooted, still dressed in her apprentice clothes; her eyes were clear, and her brows were highly arched on her fine curved white forehead, framed by straight, dark chestnut hair, which in the distance looked black. Tanechka's voice was clear, even, sweet, insinuating, and if one could have heard its sound only, and not given heed to the words, it would have given the impression that she was paying Alexandra Ivanovna compliments.

The other seamstresses laughed, the apprentices chuckled, they covered their faces with their black aprons and cast side glances at Alexandra Ivanovna. As for Alexandra Ivanovna, she was livid with rage.

"Wretch!" she exclaimed. "I will pull your ears for you! I won't leave a hair on your head."

Tanechka replied in a gentle voice:

"The paws are a trifle short... The poodle bites as well as barks... It may be necessary to buy a muzzle."

Alexandra Ivanovna made a movement towards Tanechka. But before Tanechka had time to lay aside her work and get up, the mistress of the establishment, a large, serious-looking woman, entered, rustling her dress.

She said sternly: "Alexandra Ivanovna, what do you mean by making such a fuss?"

Alexandra Ivanovna, much agitated, replied: "Irina Petrovna, I wish you would forbid her to call me a dog!"

Tanechka in her turn complained: "She is always snarling at something or other. Always quibbling at the smallest trifles."

But the mistress looked at her sternly and said: "Tanechka, I can see through you. Are you sure you didn't begin? You needn't think that because you are a seamstress now you are an important person. If it weren't for your mother's sake—"

Tanechka grew red, but preserved her innocent and affable manner. She addressed her mistress in a subdued voice: "Forgive me, Irina Petrovna, I will not do it again. But it wasn't altogether my fault . . ."

Alexandra Ivanovna returned home almost ill with rage. Tanechka had guessed her weakness.

"A dog! Well, then I am a dog," thought Alexandra Ivanovna, "but it is none of her affair! Have I looked to see whether she is a serpent or a fox? It is easy to find one out, but why make a fuss about it? Is a dog worse than any other animal?"

The clear summer night languished and sighed, a soft breeze from the adjacent fields occasionally blew down the peaceful streets. The moon rose clear and full, that very same moon which rose long ago at another place, over the broad desolate steppe, the home of the wild, of those who ran free, and whined in their ancient earthly travail. The very same, as then and in that region.

And now, as then, glowed eyes sick with longing; and her heart, still wild, not forgetting in town the great spaciousness of the steppe, felt oppressed; her throat was troubled with a tormenting desire to howl like a wild thing.

She was about to undress, but what was the use? She could not sleep, anyway.

She went into the passage. The warm planks of the floor bent and creaked under her, and small shavings and sand which covered them tickled her feet not unpleasantly.

She went out on to the doorstep. There sat the *babushka*

Stepanida, a black figure in her black shawl, gaunt and shrivelled. She sat with her head bent, and it seemed as though she were warming herself in the rays of the cold moon.

Alexandra Ivanovna sat down beside her. She kept looking at the old woman sideways. The large curved nose of her companion seemed to her like the beak of an old bird.

"A crow?" Alexandra Ivanovna asked herself.

She smiled, forgetting for the moment her longing and her fears. Shrewd as the eyes of a dog her own lighted up with the joy of her discovery. In the pale green light of the moon the wrinkles of her faded face became altogether invisible, and she seemed once more young and merry and light-hearted, just as she was ten years ago, when the moon had not yet called upon her to bark and bay of nights before the windows of the dark bathhouse.

She moved closer to the old woman, and said affably: "*Babushka* Stepanida, there is something I have been wanting to ask you."

The old woman turned to her, her dark face furrowed with wrinkles, and asked in a sharp, oldish voice that sounded like a caw: "Well, my dear? Go ahead and ask."

Alexandra Ivanovna gave a repressed laugh; her thin shoulders suddenly trembled from a chill that ran down her spine.

She spoke very quietly: "*Babushka* Stepanida, it seems to me—tell me is it true?—I don't know exactly how to put it—but you, *babushka*, please don't take offence—it is not from malice that I—"

"Go on, my dear, never fear, say it," said the old woman.

She looked at Alexandra Ivanovna with glowing, penetrating eyes.

"It seems to me, *babushka*—please, now, don't take offence—as though you, *babushka*, were a crow."

The old woman turned away. She was silent and merely nodded her head. She had the appearance of one who had recalled something. Her head, with its sharply outlined nose, bowed and nodded, and at last it seemed to Alexandra Ivanovna that the old woman was dozing. Dozing, and mumbling something under her nose. Nodding her head and mumbling some old forgotten words—old magic words.

An intense quiet reigned out of doors. It was neither light nor dark, and everything bewitched with the inarticulate mumbling of old forgotten words. Everything languished and seemed lost in apathy. Again a longing oppressed her heart. And it was neither a dream nor an illusion. A thousand perfumes, imperceptible by day, became subtly distinguishable, and they recalled something ancient and primitive, something forgotten in the long ages.

In a barely audible voice the old woman mumbled: "Yes, I am a crow. Only I have no wings. But there are times when I caw, and I caw, and tell of woe. And I am given to forebodings, my dear; each time I have one I simply must caw. People are not particularly anxious to hear me. And when I see a doomed person I have such a strong desire to caw."

The old woman suddenly made a sweeping movement with her arms, and in a shrill voice cried out twice: "Kar-r, Kar-r!"

Alexandra Ivanovna shuddered, and asked: *"Babushka,* at whom are you cawing?"

The old woman answered: "At you, my dear—at you."

It had become too painful to sit with the old woman any longer. Alexandra Ivanovna went to her own room. She sat down before the open window and listened to two voices at the gate.

"It simply won't stop whining!" said a low and harsh voice.

"And uncle, did you see—?" asked an agreeable young tenor.

Alexandra Ivanovna recognised in this last the voice of the curly-headed, somewhat red, freckled-faced lad who lived in the same court.

A brief and depressing silence followed. Then she heard a hoarse and harsh voice say suddenly: "Yes, I saw. It's very large—and white. Lies near the bath-house, and bays at the moon."

The voice gave her an image of the man, of his shovel-shaped beard, his low, furrowed forehead, his small, piggish eyes, and his spread-out fat legs.

"And why does it bay, uncle?" asked the agreeable voice.

And again the hoarse voice did not reply at once.

"Certainly to no good purpose—and where it came from is more than I can say."

"Do you think, uncle, it may be a werewolf?" asked the agreeable voice.

"I should not advise you to investigate," replied the hoarse voice.

She could not quite understand what these words implied, nor did she wish to think of them. She did not feel inclined to listen further. What was the sound and significance of human words to *her*?

The moon looked straight into her face, and persistently called her and tormented her. Her heart was restless with a dark longing, and she could not sit still.

Alexandra Ivanovna quickly undressed herself. Naked, all white, she silently stole through the passage; she then opened the outer door—there was no one on the step or outside—and ran quickly across the court and the vegetable garden, and reached the bath-house. The sharp contact of her body with the cold air and her feet with the cold ground gave her pleasure. But soon her body was warm.

She lay down in the grass, on her stomach. Then, raising herself on her elbows, she lifted her face towards the pale, brooding moon, and gave a long-drawn-out whine.

"Listen, uncle, it is whining," said the curly-haired lad at the gate.

The agreeable tenor voice trembled perceptibly.

"Whining again, the accursed one," said the hoarse, harsh voice slowly.

They rose from the bench. The gate latch clicked.

They went silently across the courtyard and the vegetable garden, the two of them. The older man, black-bearded and powerful, walked in front, a gun in his hand. The curly-headed lad followed tremblingly, and looked constantly behind.

Near the bath-house in the grass, lay a huge white dog, whining piteously. Its head, black on the crown, was raised to the moon, which pursued its way in the cold sky; its hind legs were strangely thrown backward, while the front ones, firm and straight, pressed hard against the ground.

In the pale green and unreal light of the moon it seemed enormous, so huge a dog was surely never seen on earth. It was thick and fat. The black spot, which began at the head and stretched in uneven strands down the entire spine, seemed like a woman's loosened hair. No tail was visible, presumably it was turned under. The fur on the body was so short that in the distance the dog seemed wholly naked, and its hide shone dimly in the moonlight, so that altogether it resembled the body of a nude woman, who lay in the grass and bayed at the moon.

The man with the black beard took aim. The curly-haired lad crossed himself and mumbled something.

The discharge of a rifle sounded in the night air. The dog gave a groan, jumped up on its hind legs, became a naked woman, who, her body covered with blood, started to run, all the while groaning, weeping and raising cries of distress. The black-bearded one and the curly-headed one threw themselves in the grass, and began to moan in wild terror.

THE HOUND

by William Faulkner

ONE OF AMERICA'S *most distinguished authors, William Harrison Faulkner (1897–1962) is best known for a cycle of novels and stories, of which* The Hound *is one, dealing with decadent aspects of the American South. His controversial themes did not immediately endear him to the literary establishment and it was not until his reputation had been made in Europe that his genius was fully recognized at home. He was the 1949 recipient of the Nobel Prize for Literature and was awarded a Pulitzer Prize in 1955.*

As far as I have been able to discover, this story has never before been published in Britain.

To Cotton the shot was the loudest thing he had ever heard in his life. It was too loud to be heard all at once. It continued to build up about the thicket, the dim, faint road, long after the hammer-like blow of the ten-gauge shotgun had shocked into his shoulder and long after the smoke of the black powder with which it was charged had dissolved, and after the maddened horse had whirled twice and then turned galloping, diminishing, the empty stirrups clashing against the empty saddle.

It made too much noise. It was outrageous, unbelievable—a gun which he had owned for twenty years. It stunned him with amazed outrage, seeming to press him down into the thicket, so that when he could make the second shot, it was too late and the hound, too, was gone.

Then he wanted to run. He had expected that. He had

coached himself the night before. "Right after it you'll want to run," he told himself. "But you can't run. You got to finish it. You got to clean it up. It will be hard, but you got to do it. You got to set there in the bushes and shut your eyes and count slow until you can make to finish it."

He did that. He laid the gun down and sat where he had lain behind the log. His eyes were closed. He counted slowly, until he had stopped shaking and until the sound of the gun and the echo of the galloping horse had died out of his ears. He had chosen his place well. It was a quiet road, little used, marked not once in three months save by that departed horse; a short cut between the house where the owner of the horse lived and Varner's store; a quiet, fading, grass-grown trace along the edge of the river bottom empty save for the two of them, the one squatting in the bushes, the other lying on his face in the road.

Cotton was a bachelor. He lived in a chinked log cabin floored with clay on the edge of the bottom, four miles away. It was dusk when he reached home. In the well-house at the back he drew water and washed his shoes. They were not muddier than usual, and he did not wear them save in severe weather, but he washed them carefully. Then he cleaned the shotgun and washed it too, barrel and stock; why he could not have said, since he had never heard of fingerprints, and immediately afterward he picked up the gun again and carried it into the house and put it away. He kept firewood, a handful of charred pine knots, in the chimney corner. He built a fire on the clay hearth and cooked his supper and ate and went to bed. He slept on a quilt pallet on the floor; he went to bed by barring the door and removing his overalls and lying down. It was dark after the fire burned out; he lay in the darkness. He thought about nothing at all save that he did not expect to sleep. He felt no triumph, vindication, nothing. He just lay there, thinking about nothing at all, even when he began to hear the dog. Usually at night he would hear dogs, single dogs ranging alone in the bottom, or coon- or cat-hunting packs. Having nothing else to do, his life, his heredity, and his heritage centred within a five-mile radius of Varner's store. He knew almost any dog he would hear by its voice, as he knew almost any man he would hear by his voice. He knew his dog's voice. It and the galloping horse with the flapping stirrups and the owner of the horse had been inseparable: when he saw one of them, the other two would not be far away—a lean, rangy brute that charged savagely at any one who approached its master's house, with something of the master's certitude and overbearance: and today was not the first time he had tried to kill it, though only now did he know why he had not gone through with it. "I never knowed my own luck," he said to himself, lying on the pallet. "I never knowed. If I had went ahead and killed it, killed the dog..."

He was still not triumphant. It was too soon yet to be proud, vindicated. It was too soon. It had to do with death. He did not believe that a man could pick up and move that irrevocable distance at a moment's notice. He had completely forgotten about the body. So he lay with his gaunt, underfed body empty with waiting, thinking of nothing at all, listening to the dog. The cries came at measured intervals, timbrous, sourceless, with the sad, peacefully, abject quality of a single hound in the darkness, when suddenly he found himself sitting bolt upright on the pallet.

"Nigger talk," he said. He had heard (he had never known a negro himself, because of the antipathy, the economic jealousy, between his kind and negroes) how negroes claimed that a dog would howl at the recent grave of its master. "Hit's nigger talk," he said, all the time he was putting on his overalls and his recently cleaned shoes. He opened the door. From the dark river bottom below the hill on which the cabin sat the howling of the dog came, bell-like and mournful. From a nail just inside the door he took down a coiled ploughline and descended the slope.

Against the dark wall of the jungle fireflies winked and drifted; from beyond the black wall came the booming and grunting of frogs. When he entered the timber he could not see his own hand. The footing was treacherous with slime and creepers and bramble. They possessed the perversity of inanimate things, seeming to spring out of the darkness and clutch him with spiky tentacles. From the musing impenetrability ahead the voice of the hound came steadily. He followed the sound, muddy again; the air was chill, yet he was sweating. He was quite near the sound. The hound ceased. He plunged forward, his teeth drying under his dry lip, his hands clawed and blind, towards the ceased sound, the faint phosphorescent glare of the dog's eyes. The eyes vanished. He stopped, panting, stooped, the ploughline in his hand, looking for the eyes. He cursed the dog, his voice a dry whisper. He could hear silence but nothing else.

He crawled on hands and knees, telling where he was by the shape of the trees on the sky. After a time, the brambles raking and slashing at his face, he found a shallow ditch. It was rank with rotted leaves; he waded ankle-deep in the pitch darkness, in something not earth and not water, his elbow crooked before his face. He stumbled upon something, an object with a slack feel. When he touched it, something gave a choked, infantile cry, and he started back, hearing the creature scuttle away. "Just a possum," he said. "Hit was just a possum."

He wiped his hands on his flanks in order to pick up the shoulders. His flanks were foul with slime. He wiped his hands on his shirt, across his breast, then he picked up the shoulders. He walked backward, dragging it. From time to time he would stop and wipe his hands on his shirt. He stopped beside a tree, a rotting cypress shell, topless, about ten feet tall. He had put the coiled ploughline into his bosom. He knotted it about the body and climbed the stump. The top was open, rotted out. He was not a large man, not as large as the body, yet he hauled it up to him hand over hand, bumping and scraping it along the stump, until it lay across the lip like a half-filled meal sack. The knot in the rope had slipped tight. At last he took out his knife and cut the rope and tumbled the body into the hollow stump.

It didn't fall far. He shoved at it, feeling around it with his hands for the obstruction; he tied the rope about the stub of a limb and held the end of it in his hands and stood on the body and began to jump up and down upon it, whereupon it fled suddenly beneath him and left him dangling on the rope.

He tried to climb the rope, rasping off with his knuckles the rotten fibre, a faint powder of decay like snuff in his nostrils. He heard the stub about which the rope was tied crack and felt it begin to give. He leaped upward from nothing, scrabbling at the rotten wood, and got one hand over the edge. The wood crumbled beneath his fingers; he climbed perpetually without an inch of gain, his mouth cracked upon his teeth, his eyes glaring at the sky.

The wood stopped crumbling. He dangled by his hands, breathing. He drew himself up and straddled the edge. He sat there for a while. Then he climbed down and leaned against the hollow trunk.

When he reached his cabin he was tired, spent. He had never been so tired. He stopped at the door. Fireflies still blew along the dark band of timber, and owls hooted and the frogs still boomed and grunted. "I ain't never been so tired," he said, leaning against the house, the wall which he had built log by log. "Like ever' thing had got outen hand. Climbing that stump, and the noise that shot made. Like I had got to be somebody else without knowing it, in a place where noise was louder, climbing harder to climb, without knowing it." He went to bed. He took off the muddy shoes, the overalls, and lay down; it was late then. He could tell by a summer star that came into the square window at two o'clock and after.

Then, as if it had waited for him to get settled and comfortable, the hound began to howl again. Lying in the dark, he heard the first cry come up from the river bottom, mournful, timbrous, profound.

Five men in overalls squatted against the wall of Varner's store. Cotton made the sixth. He sat on the top step, his back against a gnawed post which supported the wooden awning of the veranda. The seventh man sat in the single splint chair; a fat, slow man in denim trousers and a collarless white shirt, smoking a cob pipe. He was past middle-age. He was sheriff of the county. The man about whom they were talking was named Houston.

"He hadn't no reason to run off," one said. "To disappear. To send his horse back home with a empty saddle. He hadn't no reason. Owning his own land, his house. Making a good crop every year. He was as well-fixed as ere a man in the county. A bachelor too. He hadn't no reason to disappear. You can mark it. He never run. I don't know what; but Houston never run."

"I don't know," a second said. "You can't tell what a man has got in his mind. Houston might a had a reason that we don't know, for making it look like something had happened to him. For clearing outen the country and leaving it to look like something had happened to him. It's been done before. Folks before him has had reason to light out for Texas with a changed name."

Cotton sat a little below their eyes, his face lowered beneath his worn, stained, shabby hat. He was whittling at a stick, a piece of pine board.

"But a fellow can't disappear without leaving no trace," a third said. "Can he, Sheriff?"

"Well, I don't know," the Sheriff said. He removed the cob pipe and spat neatly across the porch into the dust. "You can't tell what a man will do when he's pinched. Except it will be something you never thought of. Never counted on. But if you can find just what pinched him you can pretty well tell what he done."

"Houston was smart enough to do ere a thing he taken a notion to," the second said. "If he'd wanted to disappear, I reckon we'd a known about what we know now."

"And what's that?" the third said.

"Nothing," the second said.

"That's a fact," the first said. "Houston was a secret man."

"He wasn't the only secret man around here," a fourth said.

To Cotton it sounded sudden, since the fourth man had said no word before. He sat against the post, his hat slanted forward so that his face was invisible, believing that he could feel their eyes. He watched the silver peel slow and smooth from the stick, ahead of his worn knife blade. "I got to say something," he told himself.

"He warn't no smarter than nobody else," he said. Then he
wished he had not spoken. He could see their feet beneath his
hat brim. He trimmed the stick, watching the knife, the steady
sliver. "It's got to trim off smooth," he told himself. "It don't
dast to break." He was talking; he could hear his voice: "Swelling around like he was the biggest man in the county. Setting
that ere dog on folks' stock." He believed that he could feel their
eyes, watching their feet, watching the sliver trim smooth and
thin and unhurried beneath the knife blade. Suddenly he thought
about the gun, the loud crash, the jarring shock. "Maybe I'll
have to kill them all," he said to himself—a mild man in worn
overalls, with a gaunt face and lack-lustre eyes like a sick man,
whittling a stick with a thin hand, thinking about killing them.
"Not them: just the words, the talk." But the talk was familiar,
the intonation, the gestures; but so was Houston. He had known
Houston all his life: that prosperous and overbearing man.
"With a dog," Cotton said, watching the knife return and bite
into another sliver. "A dog that et better than me. I work, and
eat worse than his dog. If I had been his dog, I would not
have ... We're better off without him," he said, blurted. He
could feel their eyes, sober, intent.

"He always did rile Ernest," the first said.

"He taken advantage of me," Cotton said, watching the in-
fallible knife. "He taken advantage of ever man he could."

"He was an overbearing man," the Sheriff said.

Cotton believed that they were still watching him, hidden
behind their detached voices.

"Smart, though," the third said.

"He wasn't smart enough to win that suit against Ernest over
that hog."

"That's so. How much did Ernest get outen that lawing? He
ain't never told, has he?"

Cotton believed that they knew how much he had got from
the suit. The hog had come into his lot one October. He penned
it up; he tried by inquiry to find the owner. But none claimed
it until he had wintered it on his corn. In the spring Houston
claimed the hog. They went to court. Houston was awarded the

hog, though he was assessed a sum for the wintering of it, and one dollar, a pound-fee for a stray. "I reckon that's Ernest's business," the Sheriff said, after a time.

Again Cotton heard himself talking, blurting. "It was a dollar," he said, watching his knuckles whiten about the knife handle. "One dollar." He was trying to make his mouth stop talking. "After all I taken offen him . . ."

"Juries does queer things," the Sheriff said, "in little matters. But in big matters they're mostly right."

Cotton whittled, steady and deliberate. "At first you want to run," he told himself. "But you got to finish it. You got to count a hundred, if it needs, and finish it."

"I heard that dog again last night," the third said.

"You did?" the Sheriff said.

"It ain't been home since the day the horse come in with the saddle empty," the first said.

"It's out hunting, I reckon," the Sheriff said. "It'll come in when it gets hungry."

Cotton trimmed at the stick. He did not move.

"Niggers claim a hound'll howl till a dead body's found," the second said.

"I've heard that," the Sheriff said. After a time a car came up and the Sheriff got into it. The car was driven by a deputy. "We'll be late for supper," the Sheriff said. The car mounted the hill; the sound died away. It was getting towards sundown.

"He ain't much bothered," the third said.

"Why should he be?" the first said. "After all, a man can leave his house and go on a trip without telling everybody."

"Looks like he'd unsaddled that mare, though," the second said. "And there's something the matter with that dog. It ain't been home since, and it ain't treed. I been hearing it ever night. It ain't treed. It's howling. It ain't been home since Tuesday. And that was the day Houston rid away from the store here on that mare."

Cotton was the last one to leave the store. It was after dark when he reached home. He ate some cold bread and loaded the shotgun and sat beside the open door until the hound began to howl. Then he descended the hill and entered the bottom.

The dog's voice guided him; after a while it ceased, and he saw its eyes. They were not motionless; in the red glare of the explosion he saw the beast entire in sharp relief. He saw it in the act of leaping into the ensuing welter of darkness; he heard the thud of its body. But he couldn't find it. He looked carefully, quartering back and forth, stopping to listen. But he had seen the shot strike it and hurl it backward, and he turned aside for about a hundred yards in the pitch darkness and came to a slough. He flung the shotgun into it, hearing the sluggish splash, watching the vague water break and recover, until the last ripple fled. He went home and to bed.

He didn't go to sleep though, although he knew he would not hear the dog. "It's dead," he told himself, lying on his quilt pallet in the dark. "I saw the bullets knock it down. I could count the shots. The dog is dead." But still he did not sleep. He did not need to sleep; he did not feel tired or stale in the mornings, though he knew it was not the dog. So he took to spending the nights sitting up in a chair in the door, watching the fireflies and listening to the frogs and the owls.

He entered Varner's store. It was in mid-afternoon; the porch was empty, save for the clerk, whose name was Snopes. "Been looking for you for two-three days," Snopes said. "Come inside."

Cotton entered. The store smelled of cheese and leather and new earth. Snopes went behind the counter and reached from under the counter a shotgun. It was caked with mud. "This is yourn' ain't it?" Snopes said. "Vernon Tull said it was. A nigger squirl hunter found it in a slough."

Cotton came to the counter and looked at the gun. He did not touch it; he just looked at it. "It ain't mine," he said.

"Ain't nobody around here got one of them old Hadley tengauges except you," Snopes said. "Tull says it's yourn."

"It ain't none of mine," Cotton said. "I got one like it. But mine's to home."

Snopes lifted the gun. He breeched it. "It had one empty and one load in it," he said. "Who you reckon it belongs to?"

"I don't know," Cotton said. "Mine's to home." He had come to purchase food. He bought it: crackers, cheese, a tin of sardines. It was not dark when he reached home, yet he opened the sardines and ate his supper. When he lay down he did not even remove his overalls. It was as though he waited for something, stayed dressed to move and go at once. He was still waiting for whatever it was when the window turned grey and then yellow and then blue; when, framed by the square window, he saw against the fresh morning a single soaring speck. By sunrise there were three of them, and then seven.

All that day he watched them gather, wheeling and wheeling, drawing their concentric black circles, watching the lower ones wheel down and down and disappear below the trees. He thought it was the dog. "They'll be through by noon," he said. "It wasn't a big dog."

When noon came they had not gone away; there were still more of them, while still the lower ones dropped down and disappeared below the trees. He watched them until dark came, until they were away, flapping singly and sluggishly up from beyond the trees. "I got to eat," he said. "With the work I got to do tonight." He went to the hearth and knelt and took up a pine knot, and he was kneeling, nursing a match into flame, when he heard the hound again; the cry deep, timbrous, unmistakable, and sad. He cooked his supper and ate.

With his axe in his hand he descended through his meagre corn patch. The cries of the hound could have guided him, but he did not need it. He had not reached the bottom before he believed that his nose was guiding him. The dog still howled. He paid it no attention, until the beast sensed him and ceased, as it had done before; again he saw its eyes. He paid no attention to them. He went to the hollow cypress trunk and swung his axe into it, the axe sinking helve-deep into the rotten wood. While he was tugging at it something flowed silent and savage out of the darkness behind him and struck him a slashing blow. The axe had just come free; he fell with the axe in his hand, feeling the hot reek of the dog's breath on his face and hearing the click of its teeth as he struck it down with his free hand. It leaped again; he saw its eyes now. He was on his knees, the axe raised in both hands now. He swung it, hitting nothing, feeling nothing; he saw the dog's eyes, crouched. He rushed at the eyes; they vanished. He waited a moment, but heard nothing. He returned to the tree.

At the first stroke of the axe the dog sprang at him again. He was expecting it, so he whirled and struck with the axe at the two eyes and felt the axe strike something and whirl from his hands. He heard the dog whimper, he could hear it crawling away. On his hands and knees he hunted for the axe until he found it.

He began to chop at the base of the stump, stopping between blows to listen. But he heard nothing, saw nothing. Overhead the stars were swinging slowly past; he saw the one that looked into his window at two o'clock. He began to chop steadily at the base of the stump.

The wood was rotten; the axe sank helve-deep at each stroke, as into sand or mud; suddenly Cotton knew that it was not imagination he smelled. He dropped the axe and began to tear at the rotten wood with his hands. The hound was beside him, whimpering; he did not know it was there, not even when it thrust its head into the opening, crowding against him, howling.

"Git away," he said, still without being conscious that it was the dog. He dragged at the body, feeling it slough upon its own bones, as though it were too large for itself; he turned his face away, his teeth glared, his breath furious and outraged and restrained. He could feel the dog surge against his legs, its head in the orifice, howling.

When the body came free, Cotton went over backwards. He lay on his back on the wet ground, looking up at a faint patch of starry sky. "I ain't never been so tired," he said. The dog was howling, with an abject steadiness. "Shut up," Cotton said. "Hush. Hush." The dog didn't hush. "It'll be daylight soon," Cotton said to himself. "I got to get up."

He got up and kicked at the dog. It moved away, but when he stooped and took hold of the legs and began to back away, the dog was there again, moaning to itself. When he would stop to rest, the dog would howl again; he kicked at it. Then it began to be dawn, the trees coming spectral and vast out of the miasmic darkness. He could see the dog plainly. It was gaunt, thin, with a long bloody gash across its face. "I'll have to get shut of you," he said. Watching the dog, he stooped and found a stick. It was rotten, foul with slime. He clutched it. When the hound lifted its muzzle to howl, he struck. The dog whirled; there was a long fresh scar running from shoulder to flank. It leaped at him, without a sound; he struck again. The stick took it fair between the eyes. He picked up the ankles and tried to run.

It was almost light. When he broke through the undergrowth upon the river bank the channel was invisible; a long bank of what looked like cotton batting, though he could hear the water beneath it somewhere. There was a freshness here; the edges of the mist licked into curling tongues. He stooped and lifted the body and hurled it into the bank of mist. At the instant of vanishing he saw it—a sluggish sprawl of three limbs instead of four, and he knew why it had been so hard to free from the stump. "I'll have to make another trip," he said; then he heard a pattering rush behind him. He didn't have time to turn when the hound struck him and knocked him down. It didn't pause. Lying on his back, he saw it in mid-air like a bird, vanish into the mist with a single short, choking cry.

He got to his feet and ran. He stumbled and caught himself and ran again. It was full light. He could see the stump and the black hole which he had chopped in it; behind him he could hear the swift, soft feet of the dog. As it sprang at him he stumbled and fell and saw it soar over him, its eyes like two cigar-coals; it whirled and leaped at him again before he could rise. He struck at its face with his bare hands and began to run. Together they reached the tree. It leaped at him again, slashing his arms as he ducked into the tree, seeking that member of the body which he did not know was missing until after he had released it into the mist, feeling the dog surging about his legs. Then the dog was gone. Then a voice said:

"We got him. You can come out, Ernest."

The county seat was fourteen miles away. They drove to it in a battered Ford. On the back seat Cotton and the Sheriff sat, their inside wrists locked together by handcuffs. They had to drive for two miles before they reached the high road. It was hot, ten o'clock in the morning. "You want to swap sides out of the sun?" the Sheriff said.

"I'm all right," Cotton said.

At two o'clock they had a puncture. Cotton and the Sheriff sat under a tree while the driver and the second deputy went across a field and returned with a glass jar of buttermilk and some cold food. They ate, repaired the tyre, and went on.

When they were within three or four miles of town, they began to pass wagons and cars going home from market day in town, the wagon teams plodding homeward in their own inescapable dust. The Sheriff greeted them with a single gesture of his fat arm. "Home for supper, anyway," he said. "What's the matter, Ernest? Feeling sick? Here, Joe; pull up a minute."

"I'll hold my head out," Cotton said. "Never mind." The car went on. Cotton thrust his head out the V strut of the top stanchion. The Sheriff shifted his arm, giving him play. "Go on," Cotton said, "I'll be all right." The car went on. Cotton slipped a little farther down in the seat. By moving his head a little he could wedge his throat into the apex of the iron V, the uprights gripping his jaws beneath the ears. He shifted again until his head was tight in the vise, then he swung his legs over the door, trying to bring the weight of his body sharply down against his imprisoned neck. He could hear his vertebrae; he felt a kind of rage at his own toughness; he was struggling then against the jerk on the manacle, the hands on him.

Then he was lying on his back beside the road, with water on his face and in his mouth, though he could not swallow. He couldn't speak, trying to curse, cursing in no voice. Then he was in the car again, on the smooth street where children played in the big, shady yards in small, bright garments, and men and women went home towards supper, to plates of food and cups of coffee in the long twilight of summer.

They had a doctor for him in his cell. When the doctor had

gone he could smell supper cooking somewhere—ham and hot bread and coffee. He was lying on a cot; the last ray of copper sunlight slid through a narrow window, stippling the bars upon the wall above his head. His cell was near the common room, where the minor prisoners lived, the ones who were in jail for minor offences or for three meals a day; the stairway from below came up into that room. It was occupied for the time by a group of negroes from the chain-gang that worked the streets, in jail for vagrancy or for selling a little whisky or shooting craps for ten or fifteen cents. One of the negroes was at the window above the street, yelling down to someone. The others talked among themselves, their voices rich and murmurous, mellow and singsong. Cotton rose and went to the door of his cell and held to the bars, looking at the negroes.

"Hit," he said. His voice made no sound. He put his hand to his throat; he produced a dry croaking sound, at which the negroes ceased talking and looked at him, their eyeballs rolling. "It was all right," Cotton said, "until it started coming to pieces on me. I could a handled that dog." He held his throat, his voice harsh, dry, and croaking. "But it started coming to pieces on me . . ."

"Who him?" one of the negroes said. They whispered among themselves, watching him, their eyeballs white in the dusk.

"It would a been all right," Cotton said, "but it started coming to pieces . . ."

"Hush up, white man," one of the negroes said. "Don't you be telling us no truck like that."

"Hit would a been all right," Cotton said, his voice harsh, whispering. Then it failed him again altogether. He held to the bars with one hand, holding his throat with the other, while the negroes watched him, huddled, their eyeballs white and sober. Then with one accord they turned and rushed across the room, towards the staircase; he heard slow steps and then he smelled food, and he clung to the bars, trying to see the stairs. "Are they going to feed them niggers before they feed a white man?" he said, smelling the coffee and the ham.

THE EMISSARY

by Ray Bradbury

"POETIC" IS THE *word inevitably seized upon by enthusiastic critics when reviewing the work of American Ray Bradbury. His beautifully-structured stories won him the admiration, when still in his early twenties, of established writers such as Christopher Isherwood and, without a doubt, no author has done more to help Science Fiction and Fantasy achieve literary acceptability than has Ray Bradbury. In addition to many fine classics of SF such as* The Martian Chronicles, *he wrote the screenplay for the John Huston production of* Moby Dick. *Two of his books,* Fahrenheit 451 *and* The Illustrated Man, *have likewise been filmed.*

The Emissary, *one of Ray Bradbury's earlier stories, is taken from* The October Country, *his masterly collection of weird fantasies of a kind he now writes all too rarely.*

Martin knew it was autumn again, for Dog ran into the house bringing wind and frost and a smell of apples turned to cider under trees. In dark clock-springs of hair, Dog fetched goldenrod, dust of farewell-summer, acorn-husk, hair of squirrel, feather of departed robin, sawdust from fresh-cut cordwood, and leaves like charcoals shaken from a blaze of maple trees. Dog jumped. Showers of brittle fern, blackberry vine, marshgrass spring over the bed where Martin shouted. No doubt, no doubt of it at all, this incredible beast was October!

"Here, boy, here!"

And Dog settled to warm Martin's body with all the bonfires and subtle burnings of the season, to fill the room with soft or heavy, wet or dry odours of far-travelling. In spring, he smelled of lilac, iris, lawn-mowered grass; in summer, ice-cream-moustached, he came pungent with firecracker, Roman candle, pinwheel, baked by the sun. But autumn! Autumn!

"Dog, what's it like outside?"

And lying there, Dog told as he always told. Lying there, Martin found autumn as in the old days before sickness bleached him white on his bed. Here was his contact, his carry-all, the quick-moving part of himself he sent with a yell to run and return, circle and scent, collect and deliver the time and texture of worlds in town, country, by creek, river, lake, down-cellar, up-attic, in closet or coal-bin. Ten dozen times a day he was gifted with sunflower seed, cinderpath, milkweed, horse-chestnut, or full flame-smell of pumpkin. Through the loomings of the universe Dog shuttled; the design was hid in his pelt. Put out your hand, it was there . . .

"And where did you go this morning?"

But he knew without hearing where Dog had rattled down hills where autumn lay in cereal crispness, where children lay in funeral pyres, in rustling heaps, the leaf-buried but watchful dead, as Dog and the world blew by. Martin trembled his fingers, searched the thick fur, read the long journey. Through stubbled fields, over glitters of ravine creek, down marbled spread of cemetery yard, into woods. In the great season of spices and rare incense, now Martin ran through his emissary, around, about, and home!

The bedroom door opened.

"That dog of yours is in trouble again."

Mother brought in a tray of fruit salad, cocoa, and toast, her blue eyes snapping.

"Mother . . ."

"Always digging places. Dug a hole in Miss Tarkin's garden this morning. She's spittin' mad. That's the fourth hole he's dug there this week."

"Maybe he's looking for something."

"Fiddlesticks, he's too darned curious. If he doesn't behave he'll be locked up."

Martin looked at this woman as if she were a stranger. "Oh, you wouldn't do that! How would I learn anything? How would I find things out if Dog didn't tell me?"

Mom's voice was quieter. "Is that what he does—tell you things?"

"There's nothing I don't know when he goes out and around and back, *nothing* I can't find out from him!"

They both sat looking at Dog and the dry strewings of mould and seed over the quilt.

"Well, if he'll just stop digging where he shouldn't, he can run all he wants," said Mother.

"Here, boy, here!"

And Martin snapped a tin note to the dog's collar:

MY OWNER IS MARTIN SMITH—TEN YEARS OLD—SICK IN BED—VISITORS WELCOME.

Dog barked. Mother opened the downstairs door and let him out.

Martin sat listening.

Far off and away you could hear Dog in the quiet autumn rain that was falling now. You could hear the barking-jingling fade, rise, fade again as he cut down alley, over lawn, to fetch back Mr Holloway and the oiled metallic smell of the delicate snowflake-interiored watches he repaired in his home shop. Or maybe he would bring Mr Jacobs, the grocer, whose clothes were rich with lettuce, celery, tomatoes, and the secret tinned and hidden smell of the red demons stamped on cans of devilled ham. Mr Jacobs and his unseen pink-meat devils waved often from the yard below. Or Dog brought Mr Jackson, Mrs Gillespie, Mr Smith, Mrs Holmes, *any* friend or near-friend, encountered, concerned, begged, worried, and at last shepherded home for lunch, or tea-and-biscuits.

Now, listening, Martin heard Dog below, with footsteps moving in a light rain behind him. The downstairs bell rang, Mom opened the door, light voices murmured. Martin sat forward, face shining. The stair treads creaked. A young woman's voice laughed quietly. Miss Haight, of course, his teacher from school!

The bedroom door sprang open.

Martin had company.

Morning, afternoon, evening, dawn and dusk, sun and moon circled with Dog, who faithfully reported temperatures of turf and air, colour of earth and tree, consistency of mist or rain, but—most important of all—brought back again and again and again—Miss Haight.

On Saturday, Sunday and Monday she baked Martin orange-iced cupcakes, brought him library books about dinosaurs and cavemen. On Tuesday, Wednesday and Thursday somehow he beat her at dominoes, somehow she lost at draughts, and soon, she cried, he'd defeat her handsomely at chess. On Friday, Saturday and Sunday they talked and never stopped talking, and she was so young and laughing and handsome and her hair was a soft, shining brown like the season outside the window, and she walked clear, clean and quick, a heart-beat warm in the bitter afternoon when he heard it. Above all, she had the secret of signs, and could read and interpret Dog and the symbols she searched out and plucked forth from his coat with her miraculous fingers. Eyes shut, softly laughing, in a gypsy's voice, she divined the world from the treasures in her hands.

And on Monday afternoon, Miss Haight was dead.

Martin sat up in bed, slowly.

"Dead?" he whispered.

Dead, said his mother, yes, dead, killed in a car accident a mile out of town. Dead, yes, dead, which meant cold to Martin, which meant silence and whiteness and winter come long before its time. Dead, silent, cold, white. The thoughts circled round, blew down, and settled in whispers.

Martin held Dog, thinking; turned to the wall. The lady with the autumn-coloured hair. The lady with the laughter that was very gentle and never made fun and the eyes that watched your mouth to see everything you ever said. The-other-half-of-autumn-lady, who told what was left untold by Dog, about the world. The heartbeat at the still centre of grey afternoon. The heartbeat fading . . .

"Mom? What do they do in the graveyard, Mom, under the ground? Just lay there?"

"*Lie* there."

"Lie there? Is that *all* they do? It doesn't sound like much fun."

"For goodness sake, it's not made out to be fun."

"Why don't they jump up and run around once in a while if they get tired lying there? God's pretty silly—"

"Martin!"

"Well, you'd think He'd treat people better than to tell them to lie still for keeps. That's impossible. Nobody can do it! I tried once. Dog tries. I tell him, 'dead Dog!' He plays dead awhile, then gets sick and tired and wags his tail or opens one eye and looks at me, bored. Boy, I bet sometimes those graveyard people do the same, huh, Dog?"

Dog barked.

"Be still with that kind of talk!" said Mother.

Martin looked off into space.

"Bet that's exactly what they do," he said.

Autumn burnt the trees bare and ran Dog still farther around, fording creek, prowling graveyard as was his custom, and back in the dusk to fire off volleys of barking that shook windows wherever he turned.

In the late last days of October, Dog began to act as if the wind had changed and blew from a strange country. He stood quivering on the porch below. He whined, his eyes fixed at the empty land beyond town. He brought no visitors for Martin. He stood for hours each day, as if leashed, trembling, then shot away straight, as if someone had called. Each night, he returned later, with no one following. Each night, Martin sank deeper and deeper in his pillow.

"Well, people are busy," said Mother. "They haven't time to notice the tag Dog carries. Or they mean to come to visit, but forget."

But there was more to it than that. There was the fevered shining in Dog's eyes, and his whimpering tic late at night, in some private dream. His shivering in the dark, under the bed.

The way he sometimes stood half the night, looking at Martin as if some great and impossible secret was his and he knew no way to tell it save by savagely thumping his tail, or turning in endless circles, never to lie down, spinning and spinning again.

On October 30th, Dog ran out and didn't come back at all, even when after supper Martin heard his parents call and call. The hour grew late, the streets and pavements stood empty, the air moved cold about the house and there was nothing, nothing.

Long after midnight, Martin lay watching the world beyond the cool, clear glass windows. Now there was not even autumn, for there was no Dog to fetch it in. There would be no winter, for who could bring the snow to melt in your hands? Father, Mother? No, not the same. They couldn't play the game with its special secrets and rules, its sounds and pantomimes. No more seasons. No more time. The go-between, the emissary, was lost to the wild throngings of civilization, poisoned, stolen, hit by a car, left somewhere in a culvert . . .

Sobbing, Martin turned his face to his pillow. The world was a picture under glass, untouchable. The world was dead.

Martin twisted in bed and in three days the last Hallowe'en pumpkins were rotting in trash cans, papier-mache skulls and witches were burnt on bonfires, and ghosts were stacked on shelves with other linens until next year.

To Martin, Hallowe'en had been nothing more than one evening when tin horns cried off in the cold autumn stars, children blew like goblin leaves along the flinty walks, flinging their heads, or cabbages, at porches, soap-writing names or similar magic symbols on icy windows. All of it as distant, unfathomable, and nightmarish as a puppet show seen from so many miles away that there is no sound or meaning.

For three days in November, Martin watched alternate light and shadow sift across his ceiling. The fire-pageant was over for ever; autumn lay in cold ashes. Martin sank deeper, yet deeper in white marble layers of bed, motionless, listening, always listening . . .

Friday evening, his parents kissed him good-night and walked out of the house into the hushed cathedral weather towards a motion-picture show. Miss Tarkins from next door stayed on in the parlour below until Martin called down he was sleepy, then took her knitting off home.

In silence, Martin lay following the great move of stars down a clear and moonlit sky, remembering nights such as this when he'd spanned the town with Dog ahead, behind, around about, tracking the green-plush ravine, lapping slumbrous streams gone milky with the fullness of the moon, leaping cemetery tomb-stones while whispering the marble names; on, quickly on, through shaved meadows where the only motion was the off-on quivering of stars, to streets where shadows would not stand aside for you but crowded all the pavements for mile on mile. Run now run! chasing, being chased by bitter smoke, fog, mist, wind, ghost of mind, fright of memory; home, safe, sound, snug-warm, asleep . . .

Nine o'clock.

Chime. The drowsy clock in the deep stairwell below. Chime.

Dog, come home, and run the world with you. Dog, bring a thistle with frost on it, or bring nothing else but the wind. Dog, where *are* you? Oh, listen, now, I'll call.

Martin held his breath.

Way off somewhere—a sound.

Martin rose up, trembling.

There, again—the sound.

So small a sound, like a sharp needle-point brushing the sky long miles and many miles away.

The dreamy echo of a dog—barking.

The sound of a dog crossing fields and farms, dirt roads and rabbit paths, running, running, letting out great barks of steam, cracking the night. The sound of a circling dog which came and went, lifted and faded, opened up, shut in, moved forward, went back, as if the animal were kept by someone on a fan-tastically long chain. As if the dog were running and someone whistled under the chestnut trees, in mould-shadow, tar-shadow, moon-shadow, walking, and the dog circled back and sprang out again towards home.

Dog! Martin thought, or Dog, come home, boy! Listen, oh, listen, where you *been*? Come on, boy, make tracks!

Five, ten, fifteen minutes; near, very near, the bark, the sound. Martin cried out, thrust his feet from the bed, leaned to the window. Dog! Listen, boy! Dog! Dog! He said it over and over. Dog! Dog! Wicked Dog, run off and gone all these days! Bad Dog, good Dog, home, boy, hurry, and bring what you can!

Near now, near, up the street, barking to knock clap-board housefronts with sound, whirl iron cocks on rooftops in the moon, firing off volleys—Dog! now at the door below...

Martin shivered.

Should he run—let Dog in, or wait for Mom and Dad? Wait? Oh, God, wait? But what if Dog ran off again? No, he'd go down, snatch the door wide, yell, grab Dog in, and run upstairs so fast, laughing, crying, holding tight, that...

Dog stopped barking.

Hey! Martin almost broke the window, jerking to it.

Silence. As if someone had told Dog to hush now, hush, hush.

A full minute passed. Martin clenched his fists.

Below, a faint whimpering.

Then, slowly, the downstairs front door opened. Someone was kind enough to have opened the door for Dog. Of course! Dog had brought Mr Jacobs or Mr Gillespie or Miss Tarkins, or...

The downstairs door shut.

Dog raced upstairs, whining, flung himself on the bed.

"Dog, Dog, where've you *been*, what've you *done*! Dog, Dog!"

And he crushed Dog hard and long to himself, weeping. Dog, Dog. He laughed and shouted. Dog! But after a moment he stopped laughing and crying, suddenly.

He pulled back away. He held the animal and looked at him, eyes widening.

The odour coming from Dog was different.

It was a smell of strange earth. It was a smell of night within night, the smell of digging down deep in shadow through earth that had lain cheek by jowl with things that were long hidden and decayed. A stinking and rancid soil fell away in clods of dissolution from Dog's muzzle and paws. He had dug deep. He had dug very deep indeed. That *was* it, wasn't it? wasn't it? *wasn't* it!

What kind of message was this from Dog? What could such a message mean? The stench—the ripe and awful cemetery earth.

Dog was a bad dog, digging where he shouldn't. Dog was a good dog, always making friends. Dog loved people. Dog brought them home.

And now, moving up the dark hall stairs, at intervals, came the sound of feet, one foot dragged after the other, painfully, slowly, slowly, slowly.

Dog shivered. A rain of strange night earth fell seething on the bed.

Dog turned.

The bedroom door whispered in.

Martin had company.

THE HOUND OF PEDRO

by Robert Bloch

ROBERT BLOCH IS *best known as the author of the novel* Psycho *on which Alfred Hitchcock based his masterly suspense thriller. He began writing in his 'teens under the influence of H. P. Lovecraft and went on to become one of the most successful writers of horror and suspense, specializing in his own distinctive brand of psychological terror.*

In addition to numerous novels and short stories, Robert Bloch, who lives in Hollywood, has written many screenplays for cinema and television. His latest novel, Night World, *is being filmed by M.G.M.*

I

They said he was a wizard, that he could never die. Men whispered that he held traffic with the undead and that his swarthy servants were not of human kind. The Indians murmured their fears of his incredibly wrinkled face in which, they averred, blazed two green eyes that flamed in a manner alien to men. The padres muttered too, and hinted that no mortal could exercise the powers he controlled.

But nobody knew who Black Pedro Dominguez was, or where he had come from. Even today the peons tell their tales of the Spanish oppressor, and mumble fearfully that monstrous climax which has become a legend throughout all Sonora.

It was a spring day in Novorros; that morning of April 5th, 1717. The hot sun beat upon the adobes, the wind whirled dust amidst the cacti. The bells were tolling noon-tide in the little stone chapel of the mission. Almost it seemed as though they pealed in welcome to the little band of men that rode up through the canyon to Novorros town that noon. Indeed they might, for the shaman's drums had boomed over the western hills the night before, spreading the story of the caballero who rode with his beast of black.

The Yaqui tribesmen filled the streets, their sullen faces illumined by the light of curiosity. The padre and his two brothers of the cloth watched discreetly from the steps of the mission as Black Pedro Dominguez rode into town.

Forty men and fifty horses smoked through the dust at a gallop. Strange, shining men, faceless in iron armour, straddling snorting steeds—the Indians were curiously impressed. They knew of the *conquistadores* from tales their fathers told; they had seen horses before. But the sight of the burnished steel corselets, the sun-tipped lances, the grilled masks—these things impressed them.

The padre and his brethren were impressed, too, but by more subtle details. They noted the man that rode behind the leader, the tall, lean figure on the white pony whose garb differed curiously from the war-like raiment of his fellows. This thin rider's face was hidden not by steel but by a silken mask; he wore no helmet, but a curious turban. By this and by his light Saracenic armour the priests knew him for a Moor. A Moor of Granada—here!

Then there was the heavy figure on the bay mare, the man who sat uneasily astride as though unused to riding. He wore no helmet, but about his head was wound a scarlet neckerchief. The glitter of his squinting eyes was matched by the sparkle of the gold earrings that dangled at either side of his bearded visage. He carried neither sword nor spear, but in his bloused belt reposed a hilted cutlass, in a scabbard that shone with jewels. The padre recognized him, for he had crossed the Caribbean in a galleon long years ago. This man was a buccaneer.

There were other unusual features which the white men observed while the Yaquis remained in ignorance, but there were two things which both groups noticed, two objects which impressed: Black Pedro Dominguez and his hound.

Had anyone present known of the legend, the comparison would have been irresistible, for Pedro Dominguez was seated on his horse like a malignant Buddha. He was a hog in armour, a swarthy, bearded hog whose porcine jowls were surmounted by a splayed nose and the skull-shadowed eyes of a more carnivorous beast. His forehead was a livid scar; he had been branded there by slave-irons, it seemed. There was something impressive about the man's very obscene ugliness; he *was* Buddha, but Buddha turned demon.

The natives felt it, the priests felt it. Here was evil in man.

Then they saw the hound. A great black shape loped at the heels of Pedro's horse. Huge as a cougar, supple as a panther, black as the velvet of midnight; this was the hound of Pedro. Yellow claws gleamed in the ink of great splayed paws; dark muscles rippled across the enormous belly. The lion-head was jewelled with ruby eyes, and the great slavering jaws opened on a fanged red maw that gaped in hideous hunger.

The natives felt it, the priest·felt it. Here was evil in beast.

Black Pedro Dominguez and his hound rode through the town. The cavalcade halted at the mission steps. The priest raised his hands in benediction as Pedro dismounted and stood before him.

The band had travelled far. There was foam on the horses' flanks and dust upon the armour of their riders. Sweat oozed across Black Pedro's scarred forehead. The hound cowered at his feet, moaning, with its tongue lolling like a red serpent.

Therefore as Pedro approached, the padre opened his mouth to invite him into the mission; rest, food, water might be provided.

Before he could speak, Black Pedro growled a greeting. He, he informed the padre, was Pedro Dominguez of Mexico City. He wished nothing from the good father save that he should immediately pronounce the prayers for the dead.

"What is this, sir?" the padre asked. "Can it be that you

carry with you the body of some poor man who died unshriven in the desert?"

"No," said Pedro, curtly. "But get along with the prayer." His dark eyes smouldered.

"But I do not understand," the priest continued. "Who is this prayer for?"

"For you—you fool!" Pedro smiled, grim mirth flaming in his eyes. "For you!"

It happened very quickly then. Even as he spoke, Pedro's sabre had leaped from the scabbard, risen in Pedro's hand, and descended in flashing fury on the priest's neck. There was a thud and the padre's body lay in red dust. There was a puddle in the little space between head and neck.

Others had seized the two brethren. Daggers flashed in silver sunlight. The black-gowned men dropped beside their superior.

The Yaquis stood silent. Then a vast murmuring arose, a muffled drone of anger. These strangers had killed the white brothers. Knives and bows appeared in brown hands. The tall natives closed in on the mission steps, converging in a red wave.

As if by premeditated signal the little band of whites grouped themselves in a semi-circle. Pistols appeared. And as the tribesmen closed in, flame burst upon them. A score dropped, screaming. Another belch of fire. Brown bodies writhed in agony on the dusty ground. The natives turned and fled up the adobe-lined street. The whites remounted, wheeled their steeds, and levelled their lances. Steel shivered through the retreating backs. Swords hacked at heads and shoulders. There were screams and imprecations; horses whinnied and armour clanged. But above all was the sound of grisly laughter as Black Pedro sat quaking on the mission steps. Beside him was the great hound. As the beast began to worry the bodies of the young tribesmen, Pedro laughed anew.

2

The truce came soon. The Yaquis dragged away the bodies of their slain. Gomez, the mestizo chieftain, parleyed in the mission chapel with Pedro that evening. When he heard Pedro's terms—his command—the old Indian's grey face turned pale with sick rage. He muttered to himself of Yaztan, the great Yaqui leader to the south. Even now a messenger to Yaztan was on his way, and that champion would raise an army of thousands to march against this invader.

Pedro listened, chuckled. He beckoned to the turbaned figure of the Moor behind him. Smiling with cryptic relish, the Arab bowed and left the room. In a moment he returned, bearing a leathern saddle-bag.

Pedro placed it on the table before him. Then he faced the silent Indian.

"Yaztan," he said. "I have heard of this Yaztan, the mighty chief. Is it not true that he is said to have a ring of gold set within his nose, and has pierced his cheeks with golden bracelets?"

The Indian nodded in assent.

Pedro smiled, looked at the Yaqui without comment, and opened the bag on the table.

Something shrivelled and dry rolled out—something that held the glitter of gold about a crumbled nose and sparkled yellowly in bloodless cheeks. There were no eyes in this—the head of Yaztan.

"I have already visited your chief," Pedro purred. "Before he died he told me of this place; of its mission, and of your tribe's mines. He spoke of your gold, and by the nature of your people's ornaments I see that he spoke truly. Now, as I have said, you will mine this gold for us. You have heard my terms; think them over. Or perhaps you might join Yaztan—"

Thus began the tyranny of Black Pedro; the dreadful days of bondage about which men still whisper.

They tell how Pedro visited the crude native mines, and how he ordered them enlarged and changed so that the labours of his servants might be increased. They speak of the manner in which he conscripted all the able-bodied males of the tribe, so that the women were forced to hunt while their men-folk toiled in the mines, guarded over by the bearded white men with their flame-rods that dealt death to the disobedient and their whips that bloodied the backs of the laggard and weary. They tell also of the gold that was piled in the mission towers, of the ingot-lined chambers at the church where now Black Pedro dwelt.

They speak with shame about the usage accorded their women by Pedro and his men, of Maquila the chieftain's daughter who danced to the stroke of whips in the courtyard when she failed to please the strange dark man who rode behind Black Pedro. They whisper of young virgins who disappeared each month; for with every moon Pedro exacted the tribute of a maiden.

The dark man would come at dusk to the village and demand the girl; then she would ride away to the mission house and disappear. No one dared approach that night, though the screaming sometimes would be borne afar on the lonely wind; no one dared ask next day why the girl did not return.

There was asking at first; the chief's son came, with ten young men. And Pedro scowled at them, while his hirelings seized the youths in sight of the entire tribe. They were stripped and carried to the desert. Here Black Pedro caused holes to be dug in the sand and in these holes were lowered the bodies of the young tribesmen, and earth was heaped around so that they stood buried up to the neck.

Only their heads stood silhouetted against the sand; only their faces wreathed in wonderment and vague fear. They could not know, dared not guess their fate. Did Pedro mean to leave them here to starve and die? Would they suffer hunger, thirst, the torment of heat? Would the wheeling vultures come to feast?

The tribe watched, impassive, held in check by Pedro's crew. They saw Pedro conversing with the dark man, and the swarthy squint-eyed one with the rings in his ears. They heard Pedro whisper to the squint-eyed one, and he laughed terribly and cursed in his outlandish tongue.

Then Black Pedro motioned to his soldiers, and they forced the throng away. There were fathers, mothers, wives, children of the ten young braves in that group; they were herded back with the rest.

Ten pairs of eyes followed them—ten pairs of eyes from heads set in the sand. Hopeless, helpless eyes.

The men escorted the savages back to the village. Pedro, the dark man, and the squint-eyed lieutenant remained all alone with the buried, living heads.

What occurred in the next few hours could never be rightly known. But the Yaquis could guess. For there were terrible hintings.

Several soldiers went into the convent and presently returned carrying great wooden balls of hardened fibre. These they carried back into the desert.

The savages had seen Pedro roll these balls along the inner lawn of the convent garden at times; he and the dark man were adept at bowling.

The balls were carried with them into the desert. Perhaps that was what Pedro had whispered to make the others laugh. He might have conceived a jest.

Ten-pins. Ten heads.

The heavy wooden balls rumbled thunderously as they rolled across the flat sands. The sound of human screams rose unmistakably over the booming.

When Pedro and his companions returned it was already dark. Their faces were flushed as though from exertion. When the released tribesmen hastened out to the desert, they could find no trace of heads in the sand. The men had vanished. But in the twilight when Black Pedro returned, they had seen ominous stains on the wooden bowling-balls.

The natives asked no questions, but their scowls deepened to the impassive malignity of the savage enraged. They dared not search the spot or linger to dig up that which they suspected lay beneath the sands; dared not search because it was night.

At night, Pedro's hound was abroad. It roamed their village at will, descended even to the mines where they toiled under the lash by day. When hungry, the beast sprang on the native nearest—unless an alert white guard beat it off in time. Sometimes the guard would not bother to repulse the hound if the attacked native was old and feeble.

That hound . . .

The Yaquis feared it more than they did their vicious but human master. They began to conceive queer fancies connected with both of these oppressors. These fancies were based on their scanty knowledge of what went on behind the convent walls where Pedro and his men lived in guarded seclusion. No one entered the place save to be conducted into dungeons and torture chambers below, but rumours spread. It was guessed that Pedro's band had come from Mexico, lured by tales of mines and yellow metal. How long he would stay here none could say, but the gold was piling up daily in the chapel rooms. A few old natives had been detailed to tend it there, and they started the disturbing rumours of life within the walls.

The dark man, they said, was a shaman—a wizard. It was he who advised Pedro, the old natives whispered; and it was he who tended the torture vaults in the abandoned cellars below the former mission. Victims came from the mines; disobedient natives were taken here and "punished" before their reward of death.

But (so hinted the oldsters) they were "punished" as a wizard would chastize; they were sacrificed, and their bodies rended in terrible ways.

It was the dark man, too, that demanded the virgin every moon. She was led into the cellars, the old Indians averred, and given in sacrifice where none could see. The dark man and Black Pedro and the hound went into those depths with her, and there would be the sound of chanting and praying, the screams of the girl mingled with the baying of that sable beast.

The old ones cautiously spoke of how the hound would re-emerge after this and slink off into outer darkness, but they said Pedro and the dark man remained below for several days. When the hound returned they ventured abroad once more, to hear tales of new atrocities committed without the mission walls.

Some of the tribe believed these old ones in their mutterings. Certainly they came to fear Black Pedro and his great dog increasingly as the months went by. And the secret messengers they had sent to the south gave no word.

But even the most credulous refused to believe the wilder

stories of Pedro speaking to the dog, and the animal replying in human tongue. Nevertheless a growing panic manifested itself in tribal ranks. There was talk of fleeing, but this was impossible. Uprising was out of the question; in truth, the men with the flame-rods were not over-cruel—it was Pedro, the dark man, and the strange beast that revelled in brutality.

Panic increased the rumours so that Pedro and his hound became almost legendary figures of evil. The two were almost alike in their animal lusts; dreadful things were hinted as to the fate of the maiden taken each month—tales of bestial passion and the old shaman stories of the uses accorded virgin blood. These stories drew added colour from the almost human attributes displayed at times by the hound. If it could not talk to its master as the wildest stories reputed, it could at least understand human speech and make itself understood.

The Yaquis began to realize that on nights following the monthly ceremonies the great black hound prowled about their adobes; that it listened below windows and lurked amidst the shadows beyond their campfires.

For whenever there was midnight talk of rebellion and discontent Black Pedro knew of it, and summoned the speaker to the mission. Could it be that the beast actually *reported* these things? Or was it the wizardry of the strange dark man?

None knew the truth, but each passing day the shadow of Pedro and his hound loomed larger over all their lives. And far away the messengers sped south to spread the tale.

3

Don Manuel Digron halted his march at the head of the canyon. Signal fires smoked in the dusk, and the three emissaries were waiting as the messengers had said.

They held a secret parley in the darkness, while Don Manuel listened to the natives' story. He scowled deeply as he heard, then broached his plan of action. The Yaquis nodded, then faded away in the gloom of the twilight canyons.

The men-at-arms dismounted, encamped. Don Manuel Digron kept counsel with his aide, Diego.

"Sure it is the same man," he growled. "This is Black Pedro Dominguez of whom they speak. Friar Orspito tells me that this Pedro is long wedded to the Devil, for the Holy Inquisition seeks him even now in Mother Spain. He fled from there with the Moor, Abouri—a black wizard of Granada; men tell of their exploits. The hound Pedro rules is not an earthly thing, I warrant, if tales I've heard are true."

"What does such a man here?" Diego inquired. A frown crossed Don Manuel's lean face.

"I know not. He left Mexico City—he and his band of free-booters and gutter-rats—no doubt the smell of gold lured him across the plains to Sonora. It is always so. With gold he and his damned sorcerer can command an empire."

"Are we to turn him over to Mother Church or the civil authorities?" asked Diego.

"Neither," Manuel drawled. "We have no horses to convey forty captives across the desert, nor water and provisions to sustain them. They must be disposed of here—and if half the tales of evil magic be true, it is God's work to do this."

The Don stared at the fire for a moment, then continued.

"We may taste of necromancy tonight, Diego. The chieftains inform me that this is the eve appointed for sacrifice. A living maiden is delivered to him once each moon. I trust our arrival is timely; I do not care to ponder on the usage accorded a woman by these sorcerous swine."

The two men ate and drank.

4

Two men ate and drank within the mission walls. Black Pedro dined tonight with Abouri, the Moor; they toasted gold and goety alike from amber goblets.

There was little of speech between them, but many a glance of dark understanding. The Moor smiled after a long silence, and lifted his glass.

"Fortune!" he pledged.

Pedro sneered, his little pig-eyes sullen with discontent.

"When shall we leave this cursed hole, Abouri? I long for cities where there is no sun to dry the juices from the body; we've gold enough to ransom the kings of all the world. Why tarry?"

The Moor pursed his lips urbanely as he stroked his greying beard, and his smile was placating.

"Patience," he counselled. "Be guided by my wisdom, O brother. Was it not I who led you from the galleys to riches beyond all dreams? Did we not pledge a pact before Ahriman, your Sathanas; has not He guided us on our way?"

"True." Pedro was thoughtful.

"I have brought you wealth," pursued the Moor. "And I must have my due, as our bond with your Lucifer demands. Here we have found the blood of maidens and other useful things, and I may carry out my bargain undisturbed. That was our agreement with the Master before the Altar—wealth for you, and mantic power for me, and souls for Him."

Strange fear flooded Pedro's face.

" 'Tis a dreadful pledge," he half whispered. "Souls for Him! And at what price! For the hound frightens me, and I am afraid when the exchange is made; should anything go amiss—"

The Moor raised his hand in a gesture of restraint. "That was the bond. The hound is His; He gave it to us as an instrument to secure souls for His Devil's bondage. A few days each month is little enough to ask in return for wealth. And yours is a nature to delight in the shedding of blood."

"As a man, yes—I warrant I find pleasure enough in slaying," Pedro admitted, with utter candour. "But as the other—"

Again the Moor checked his companion's speech. "Here is the maiden now, and we must prepare for this night's work."

Two trembling natives had entered the room, pushing a bound and frightened girl before them. She struggled in her bonds once they freed her legs, but they took no heed. Bowing low, they averted their faces and ran out. The Moor rose and approached the dark, lithe figure of the Indian maiden. As his hands grasped her pinioned arms she closed her eyes in utter fear.

Black Pedro leered, laughing.

"A fine wench, indeed!" he chuckled. "Could I but—"

"No," declared the Moor, sensing his purpose. "She must remain immaculate for the sacrifice. Come."

All mirth, all desire, vanished from Pedro's face as he followed the Moor and his captive down the winding stairs to the cellar crypts below. He knew what was to happen, and he was afraid.

There was nothing to reassure him in the dungeon itself. A vast, gloomy chamber, taper-litten, it was an oddly terrifying place.

Corridors stretched off into further gloom. Here were to be found the cages and the racks for prisoners, but the Moor did not go on. Instead he proceeded down the centre of the main chamber to the farther wall, where stood a great table and two flat rocks. There had been an altar here once, but it had since been removed and the crucifix above it inverted. An inverted crescent was emblazoned against it.

The girl was placed on the table. Braziers and flares were lit; alembics lifted to the light. Bubble-glass jars were hung over the fires, and a tripod sent pungent incense through the room in swirls of spiced smoke.

Tightly the girl was bound. Strongly the basin was held. Swiftly the knife was plunged. And a shriek, a moan, then bubble, bubble, bubble, as the basin filled.

Incense added, red and yellow powders filled the basin as it hung over the tripod. Black Pedro's swarthy face was pale, and sweat spurted across his gashed brows. The Moor ignored him as he worked over the flames.

Black horror loped into the room as the great dark hound slunk purposefully down the stairs. With prescient intelligence it stalked to the farther of the two stone slabs and took its place upon it. Pedro reluctantly followed suit, mounting the second slab.

And then the Moor took up the basin, filled with red and silver bubbles that glistened in the light. And the tapers were snuffed out so that darkness fell upon the crypt, and only a strange red light flamed forth from the basin in the wizard's hands. That, and the emberous glow from the hound's deep eyes . . .

The hound lapped at the basin's contents with a long red tongue. Pedro sipped, his lips ashen with terror. The Moor stood beneath the cross and crescent in the pulsing darkness. He raised his arms in a gesture of invocation as man and beast sank into coma deep as death. Sibilantly came the wizard's prayer.

"Ahriman, Lord of Beasts and Men—"

5

His sword was crimson when Manuel Digron raced down the darkened stairs. Behind him lay nightmare; nightmare and screaming death in the black reaches of the mission walls. The men-at-arms slew swiftly, but the Yaquis remained to mangle and maim in bloody attack.

The surprise attack had been successful. The Indians and the Spaniards had converged on the mission, and the forty were slain—murdered in their beds, for the most part; though a few had put up stout resistance under the leadership of the buccaneer.

Now Don Manuel Digron sought the cellar, with Diego and his lieutenants at his heels. The torches brought light as they rounded the curve in the stairs, and for a moment Manuel stared aghast.

The dead, bloodless thing lay on the table. Before it stood a turbaned figure, rapt in prayer; and behind it the two dreadful slabs of stone, on which lay a man and a gigantic hound. The lips of the hound and the lips of the man were alike bloody. And the hound squatted in a dreadfully man-like fashion, while the man crouched. It was unnatural, that tableau.

At Manuel's descent, turmoil came. The Moor looked up and wheeled about, snatching a dagger from his scarved waist.

Manuel dodged the descending weapon and thrust his sword upward so that it pierced the dark man's belly.

Then it ripped upward dreadfully, so that a crimson-grey torrent gushed forth from the side, and the Moor dropped writhing into death.

Then Manuel advanced to the slab where Black Pedro Dominguez lay. The great swarthy man cringed and gibbered, but drew no weapon. Instead he cowered, whimpering like a beast when Manuel's sword ran him through.

Manuel turned upon the hound, but the great beast had already sprung. Two men-at-arms stood on the stairs, and it leaped for the first one's throat. He fell, and beast-jaws crunched. The mighty creature turned as the other soldier raised his lance. A great paw brushed spear and shield aside; then talons ripped into the man's face and left behind only a furrow of bleeding horror.

The hound was silent, ghastly silent; it did not growl or bay. Instead it turned and rose. On two hind legs it stood, in monstrous simulation of humanity; then it turned and raced up the stairs in frantic flight. Manuel stumbled, recovered a moment later.

The rest was never quite real to him. He lay still for but a moment, listening to the groans of the dying wizard on the crypt floor, but what he heard haunted him forever.

Babblings of black delirium ... hints of a monstrous exchange the wizard made monthly after a blood sacrifice to Ahriman ... tales of a lycanthropic pact whereby the bodies of Black Pedro and the Devil's hound held alien souls for days following the sacrifice, when the hound that was not a hound ravened forth for souls given to Satan in return for gold and gifts ... the cracked voice of the sorcerer, telling of a rite just concluded ... the monthly exchange just made through blood and prayers, and a werewolf serving Evil loosed upon the world once more to seek souls for the Master ... delirium or truth?

It was then that Manuel understood and screamed aloud as he jerked erect, glaring with horrified eyes at the feebly writhing body of the Moor. Shuddering, he whirled and sprang up the stairs in pursuit of the hound.

His soldiers met him. The Indians, they said, had captured the black beast as it raced into view from the depths. A Yaqui lay dead on the floor, his throat ribboned in mute testimony to the hound's ferocity. And now Manuel could hear drums dinning in the hills, throbbing blood-lust.

He was muttering long-forgotten prayers as he ran towards where the red glare flickered, muttering prayers as he whipped the sword from his scabbard. A Yaqui death-chant, grim and relentless, boomed out into the savage night. Then Manuel plunged over the brow of the hill—and saw.

He saw that the Yaquis had remembered the deaths of their ten young men; they had remembered the ghastly jest of Black Pedro. And since he was dead, they were repeating that jest with Pedro's hound. He saw the dark head buried in sand to its shaggy throat, heard the thunder of wooden balls as they bowled along the sand, as they plunged unerringly at the screaming horror that was their target.

Manuel fell upon the natives. Snarling curses that somehow kept him sane, he and his men drove them back with the flats of their swords. And at last, alone, Manuel dared to approach the thing in the sand—the black, jutting head that lifted its foaming muzzle to the skies as it moaned in that last agony.

But Manuel, knowing what he did, dared not look at it. The wizard's dying whispers had been too much.

He gave only a swift, furtive glance as in mercy he thrust his sword through the ruined beast-skull. And as he stabbed, his heart went icy cold. He had seen the smashed jaws move feebly in one final effort as the dazed eyes glared into his own. Then, above the muffled, triumphant thunder of the distant drums, Don Manuel heard that which confirmed all the legends and rumours of which the wizard had hinted.

Don Miguel heard the incredible voice, then collapsed beside the dying beast-head with the sound still dinning in his ears.

The hound of horror spoke.

And it moaned, *"Mercy—a prayer for the dead—for me— Black Pedro."*

THE WHINING

by Ramsey Campbell

ONE OF THE *best-received stories in my* Beware of the
Cat *anthology was* Cat and Mouse *by Ramsey Campbell,
a young writer who has attracted much attention for his
treatment of traditional fantasy themes in a highly contem-
porary and often controversial manner. His second collection of weird stories,* Demons by Daylight, *was recently
published by Arkham House and was enthusiastically re-
viewed. He is at present working on a novel, his first.*

*In the following unnerving tale, Ramsey unleashes his
Hell-hound not on some desolate wind-blasted moor but in
the suburbs of his home-town of Liverpool. And it's all the
more disturbing for having a setting we can readily identify
with.*

When Bentinck first saw the dog he thought it was a patch of
mud. He was staring from his window into Princes Park, watching the snow heap itself against folds of earth and slip softly
from branches. Against the black trees on the far side of
the park, flakes shimmered like light within the eyelids. Bentinck
gazed, trying to calm himself, and his eye was caught by a
brown heap on the gradual slope of the green.

It lanced his mood. He sighed and began to gather his coffee-
cup, smashed in a momentary rage. At least he hadn't allowed
his fury to touch the Radio Merseyside tape-recorder, which
contained its source. He opened the French windows and hurried
around the corner of the house to his bin, almost tripping over
the half-buried handle of an axe. As he returned he saw that
the brown heap was shaking snow from its plastered fur and

staring at him. It freed its legs from the snow and struggled towards him, half-engulfed at each weak leap.

Bentinck hesitated, then he shrugged flakes from his shoulders and closed the windows. After mopping the carpet he played back the tape. He'd worked at Radio Merseyside only a month, and already here he was, allowing a councillor to feed him answers which begged specific questions, those the councillor was prepared to answer. And off the tape Bentinck was absolutely and articulately opposed to capital punishment, in fact to any violence: that was what infuriated him. Well, he might as well be calm; the incident was beyond resolution. He might as well enjoy his free afternoon. He bundled his coat about him and emerged into the park.

Small cold flakes licked his cheeks. He crossed to the lake, his footsteps squeaking. Ducks creaked throatily across the silver sky, and a flurry of gulls detached themselves from the white with rusty squawks. Behind him Bentinck heard a wet slithering. He turned and saw the dog.

As soon as he met its eyes the dog changed direction. It began to sidle around him, a few feet away, curving its body into a shape like a ballerina's expression of shame. It circled him crabwise, pointing its nose towards him. It was several shades of mud, with trailing ears like scraps of floorcloth, and large eyes. Its legs were short and bent like roots, and its tail wavered vaguely. "All right, boy," Bentinck said. "Whose are you?"

He stopped towards it. At once it leapt clumsily backwards, rather as an insect might, he thought. "All right," he said, slapping his shin. It skidded to its feet and shook off a dandruff of snow. As it did so he saw that its skin was corrugated with ribs. "Food," he said, remembering a bone he'd intended to use for soup. But the dog stayed where it was, tail quivering. "Food, boy," he said, and began to tramp back to his flat.

Then the dog commenced whining like a gate in a high wind, a reiterated glissando rising across a third. "Food! Food!" shouted Bentinck, almost at the windows, and the couple in the first-floor flat peered out warily. I've been a fool once today,

Bentinck thought, and then glared up at them; their hi-fi seemed to need a good deal less sleep than he, and while he wouldn't complain unless it became intolerable he was damned if he would whisper for them. "Here, boy!" he shouted, and hurried to the refrigerator. Over the slight squeal of the door he heard the incessant cry from the park.

He tore a piece of meat from the bone and hurled it towards the dog. The animal made a gulping leap and began to claw up an explosion of snow where the meat had landed. Leaving the bone inside the window, Bentinck found a towel in his laudry-bag. In the living-room he halted, surprised. The dog was sitting in front of the gas fire, gnawing the bone. It snarled.

"Do sit down," Bentinck said. "You don't mind if I close the windows?" Out of the corner of its eye the dog watched him do so. "I don't suppose you'd consider lying on this towel. No, I thought not," he said. "Just so long as we can both have the fire." The dog grumbled as he sat down, but continued chewing. Bentinck gazed at it. Its back legs curled around and its tail followed them, as if to form a pleasing contrast to the sharp straight bone. Somehow, Bentinck thought, the contrast expressed the dog.

Gradually its jaws wound down. Bentinck had been lulled by the sight of its satiety; only the appearance of a pool seeping from beneath the animal startled him alert. Bending closer, he realized that it wasn't the thawing of the dog. "Now wait a minute," he said, springing up. The dog winced back from him, leaving the bone; it began to cringe, and its tongue and tail quivered. "All right, you poor sod, it's not your fault," he said. "I hope you don't object to the *Echo*."

But when he returned with the newspaper, the dog was scraping at the carpet and worrying the tape-recorder's lead. "I'm tempted to offer you the tape, but on balance I think you've been enough of a good deed for one day," he said. Wrapping his hand in the towel, he fished the bone out of the pool and threw it into the park. With a bark that combined a whoop with its whine, the dog followed.

Later, at Radio Merseyside, he edited the tape and had an

unpleasant slow-motion conversation with his producer. As he returned to his flat he thought he saw the dog lapping at the lake, at its encroaching margin of mud and waste paper. "I'm afraid I didn't quite manage to pin him down." "Well, you can't be expected to learn everything at once." "That's true." "But you'll have to work on mastering interviews." "Yes, I will." "Won't you." "Yes, of course." God, thought Bentinck savagely. He filled a soup-bowl with water and set it outside the windows. Under the sill the snow was flecked with blood, and there were claw-marks on the frame.

He was awakened by dull thumps overhead, which his heart continued. He dragged the alarm clock into view and saw it was four o'clock. Then he became aware of the whining, the cause of the protests resounding through the floor above. Wearily he groped his way to the French windows. As he opened them snowballs hailed down from the first floor, and the dog yelped. Indignant, Bentinck spread newspapers on the carpet and coaxed the dog inside. It slithered through the windows like a timid snake and lay down panting. "That's it, boy," Bentinck said. "Bedtime, what's left of it."

Three hours later the whining prodded him awake. "No, no, boy, shut up," he mumbled—but almost at once the dog clawed open his bedroom door and crawled towards him as if under fire, leaving a snail's trail of melted snow. He stroked its back as it came within reach, and the dog attempted to writhe itself through the carpet. Leaning over to follow his hand, Bentinck saw that the animal had an erection. It peered at him from the corner of its eye, slyly. "You go back to your own bed," Bentinck said and retreated under the blankets.

But the whining prised him forth. He opened the French windows and the dog galloped towards them, halting at his side. "I know, you're scared to go out alone," he said. "I take it I've had my sleep." He shaved, washed and dressed, trying to hush the dog. "A walk will do me the world of good," he said, opening the windows. "Jesus wept."

His feet crunched through the glazed snow and plunged into the mire of the paths. Ducks swam through a grey coating of snow. The dog ran ahead, casting itself in a curve, struggling to its feet and running back towards him. He found a dripping stick and threw it, but it only sank into banked snow with a thud. By the time they'd circled the lake his feet were soaking. He hurried inside, closing out the dog, picked up the telephone and dialled. "Didn't you use that tape? Good," he said. "I'd like to try him again." He changed his boots and left by the front door.

But the councillor had gone to Majorca for a week. When Bentinck neared home that evening, still composing questions, he hesitated at the park gates. He could go round to the front door and avoid the dog. However, he intended to take advantage of the park while its litter and mud were draped. Nothing moved on the dimming slopes. He reached his windows and unlocked them. As he did so the dog scrambled around the corner of the house and shot into his flat.

"Well, I know what *I'm* having for dinner," Bentinck said, cutting open cellophane. The dog lay on the kitchen tiles and watched him; its tail strained to rise and fell back. "You see what that says?" Bentinck said, flourishing the packet. "Dinner for one." But as he ate, his left hand secretively passed scraps of meat beneath the table, where wet teeth snapped them away.

"It's usual for guests to leave when the host shows signs of collapse," Bentinck said, tying his pyjama cord. He changed the newspapers by the windows and shivering, unlocked them. "The Gents' is outside," he said. But the dog lay down, tearing the top layer of paper. Bentinck closed the windows and his bedroom door. He set the alarm, and the whining started.

"No," he said, opening the door. "No," when the dog refused the invitation of the windows. "*No*," as it began to gaze side-long at him. Upstairs he could hear the first rumbles of displeasure. He picked up a newspaper. He'd read that a rolled-up newspaper was the kindest instrument with which to chastise a pup. He rolled the *Echo* and struck the dog's rump with the face of the year's Miss Unilever.

The dog yelped and rolled over. Then it began to fawn, curling itself about the carpet as if all its bones were broken.

It stood up in a dislocated way, its hindquarters belatedly regaining an even keel, and came towards him, licking its lips and whining. "Be quiet," he said and struck it again, harder. It spun over, almost somersaulting, and sidled back to him. Its tongue flopped out, dripping; it rubbed against his legs, swinging its tail in a great arc, and whined. "Oh, get out," he said, disgusted. "Come on. Out now." It climbed up his leg, pressing its crotch against him. "Out!" he shouted and opening the windows, picked up the struggling dog and hurled it into the snow. Then he buried himself in bed. Above him the hi-fi began to howl and thump.

For the next week he kept the windows closed. He avoided the couple on the first floor but was ready with an argument should he meet them. Each night he heard the whining and the scrape of claws on wood. On the Sunday afternoon he saw the dog ploughing through the lake in pursuit of a stick thrown by three children, which had lodged beneath a bench overturned into the lake. He watched the animal as it tried to lift the bench on its shoulders, to force itself beneath the seat, and for a moment admired the dog and envied the children. Then his mind shifted, and he wondered whether they would be able to resist the creature's temptation to sadism. He rolled up a newspaper and struck himself on the arm. He was surprised by how much it hurt.

That night the dog attacked the window while he was still reading. Bentinck rolled the paper and flourished it. The dog redoubled its efforts. One of the lower panes was scribbled with crimson, and the animal's left front paw was darker tonight. Bentinck frowned and went to bed, and in the morning called the RSPCA.

When they arrived, two men in a snarling van, the dog had vanished. Bentinck had gone to the edge of the park to entice the dog into the flat, and almost didn't hear their knocking. "Clever dog you've got there," one said, stamping the snow of the search from his boots. "Better tie him up before you ring next time." "It isn't mine," Bentinck said, but it wasn't important, and besides they were already driving away. He collected together his equipment to interview the councillor. He opened the windows, and the dog hurtled out from beneath his bed into the park.

That evening the dog wasn't waiting when he returned. He inched his way through the windows and locked them. Then, controlling himself, he made coffee. At last his hand crept forward and switched on the tape. "I'm not concerned with punishing specific criminals. I'm concerned that violence is becoming an everyday fact of life." "Now this is complete nonsense, isn't it?" he heard himself saying angrily, and switched off before his fury surfaced completely. Then the French windows began to shudder.

He stared at them. The dog was hurling itself against them, clawing at the frame. Bentinck leapt to his feet and gestured it away, but it swung its tail and began to dig at the sill. He wrenched open the windows to shove the dog away, but it had already squeezed into the room. "Come on," he said. "I don't want you." At that moment someone knocked at the door of the flat: a man with a thin frowning face and long grey hair tucked inside a car-coat. Of course, the landlord.

"I'll get my cheque-book," Bentinck said, wondering why the man was frowning.

"The people upstairs have been complaining about your dog."

"It's not my dog," Bentinck said, dropping his cheque-book. "And in any case I'm surprised they can hear it at all over their hi-fi, which they play till all hours."

"Really? It's odd you haven't complained before. Whose dog is it if it isn't yours?"

"God knows. All I know is I'd like to see the last of it."

"Do you know, I've gone through life convinced that the man's the master of the dog. What is this dog, a hypnotist?"

"No," Bentinck snarled, "a bloody pest."

"Well, I'll tell you what to do with pests, just between us. You get some meat and cook it up with poison. Simple as that. I'll even let you dig in the garden if you do it quietly. There's your rent book. I'll see myself out."

The landlord left, leaving the door ajar. I've tried the

RSPCA, Bentinck said furiously, you try them if you're so bothered. I might give them a ring about you. The dog was fawning at his feet. "Stop that," he shouted, stamping, and stood up to close the door.

Behind him there came a thud. The dog was chewing the tape-recorder lead and had pulled the machine to the floor. "Haven't I made myself clear?" Bentinck shouted. He opened the windows and stamped at the dog, herding it towards them. It crawled around the room, cringing back from furniture, trying to climb his leg, and he grasped it by the scruff of its neck and dragged it yelping towards the windows. Still holding the dog, he closed the windows behind him.

"Now go. Just go," he said, kicking slush at it. It ran splashing towards the bins, its tail wagging limply, but when he turned to the windows it began to sidle back. "Go, will you!" he shouted, running at the dog and tripping. He pushed himself to his feet, his hands gloved in ice, as the dog leapt at him and smeared his mouth with its tongue. "Go!" he shouted and fumbling behind him for what he'd tripped over, threw it.

He heard the axe strike. The dog screamed and then began to whine, its cry rising and rising. "Oh Christ," Bentinck said. There was no light from the first floor, and he couldn't see what he'd done, only make out the dog dragging itself by its front paws through the crackling slush towards the park. He couldn't do anything. He couldn't bear to touch the dog. He stumbled towards it and saw the axe cleaving the snow. Closing his eyes, he picked up the axe and killed the dog.

Afterwards he found a spade standing against the house. He had to hold the dog together while he wrapped it in polythene. Shovelling and kicking, he disguised the discoloured snow. Then he dug a hole at the edge of the park, filled it in and tried to scatter snow over the disturbed earth. For hours he lay in bed shaking.

Next morning a corner of polythene was protruding from the ground. Bentinck trod it out of sight, shuddering, feeling the ground yield beneath his heel. When he came home, having successfully edited the tape, he found a whole edge of polythene billowing from a scraped hollow. Several dogs were chasing in the park. He dug the ground over, watching for a face at the first-floor window, as the first flakes of a new snow drifted down.

He awoke to the memory of a whining. He sat up, hurling the blanket to the floor. For minutes he listened, then he padded to the French windows. The garden was calm and softened by unbroken snow. A full moon floated in the clear sky, coaxing illumination from the landscape. He returned to his bedroom. Thick darkness lay beneath the bed.

The councillor blustered. Bentinck shrugged him off and turned his back. Before him, dawning from the shadows, lay a dog or a young girl. Bentinck held scissors, a red-hot poker, an axe, a saw. He awoke writhing, soaked in sweat, an eager whining in his ears. His whole body was pounding. He let his breathing ease, and groped for the clock. Before he could reach it, a tongue licked his hand.

The couple on the first floor were awakened by shouts. Groaning, they turned over and sought sleep. At eight o'clock they were eating breakfast when they saw Bentinck staggering about the park. "He's drunk. That explains a lot," the woman said. But something in his manner made them go to his assistance. When they drew near they saw that his trouser legs were covered with dried blood. Around him in the snow the prints of dogs' paws formed wildly fragmented patterns. "Listen," he said desperately. "You realize it's impossible to exorcise an animal? They don't understand English, never mind Latin." They took his arms and began to guide him back to his flat. But they hadn't reached the house when he looked down and started to brush at his shins, and kick, and scream.

THE DEATH HOUND

by Dion Fortune

THE MYSTERIOUS-SOUNDING *name of Dion Fortune masked the identity of Violet Wirth (1890–1946), the most influential female occultist since Madame Blavatsky. A devotee of magic throughout her life, Dion Fortune joined the famous Order of the Golden Dawn in 1914 and later founded her own occult order, the Society of the Inner Light, which is still active today.*

Dion Fortune possessed remarkable mediumistic powers and in Psychic Self-Defence, *one of her many important works of magical doctrine, she describes how, following an unconscious invocation to "Fenris, the Wolf-Horror of the North", she "created" an elemental spirit in the shape of a dog: "I obtained an excellent materialization in the half-light and could have sworn that a big Alsation was standing there looking at me. It was tangible, even to the dog-like odour."*

The following story, which features her best fictional creation, the occult detective, Doctor Taverner, is also believed to have been based on one of Dion Fortune's actual psychical experiences.

"Well?" said my patient when I had finished stethoscoping him, "have I got to go softly all the days of my life?"

"Your heart is not all it might be," I replied, "but with care it ought to last as long as you want it. You must avoid all undue exertion, however."

The man made a curious grimace. "Supposing exertion seeks me out?" he asked.

"You must so regulate your life as to reduce the possibility to a minimum."

Taverner's voice came from the other side of the room. "If you have finished with his body, Rhodes, I will make a start on his mind."

"I have a notion," said our patient, "that the two are rather intimately connected. You say I must keep my body quiet"—he looked at me—"but what am I to do if my mind deliberately gives it shocks?" and he turned to my colleague.

"That is where I come in," said Taverner. "My friend has told you what to do; now I will show you how to do it. Come and tell me your symptoms."

"Delusions," said the stranger as he buttoned his shirt. "A black dog of ferocious aspect who pops out of dark corners and chivvies me, or tries to. I haven't done him the honour to run away from him yet; I daren't, my heart's too dickey, but one of these days I am afraid I may, and then I shall probably drop dead."

Taverner raised his eyes to me in a silent question. I nodded; it was quite a likely thing to happen if the man ran far or fast.

"What sort of a beast is your dog?" enquired my colleague.

"No particular breed at all. Just plain dog, with four legs and a tail, about the size of a mastiff, but not of the mastiff build."

"How does he make his appearance?"

"Difficult to say; he does not seem to follow any fixed rule, but usually after dusk. If I am out after sundown, I may look over my shoulder and see him padding along behind me, or if I am sitting in my room between daylight fading and lamp lighting, I may see him crouching behind the furniture watching his opportunity."

"His opportunity for what?"

"To spring at my throat."

"Why does he not take you unawares?"

"That is what I cannot make out. He seems to miss so many chances, for he always waits to attack until I am aware of his presence."

"What does he do then?"

"As soon as I turn and face him, he begins to close in on me! If I am out walking, he quickens his pace so as to overtake me, and if I am indoors he sets to work to stalk me round the furniture. I tell you, he may only be a product of my imagination, but he is an uncanny sight to watch."

The speaker paused and wiped away the sweat that had gathered on his forehead during this recital.

Such a haunting is not a pleasant form of obsession for any man to be afflicted with, but for one with a heart like our patient's it was peculiarly dangerous.

"What defence do you offer to this creature?" asked Taverner.

"I keep on saying to it 'You're not real, you know, you are only a beastly nightmare, and I'm not going to let myself be taken in by you.'"

"As good a defence as any," said Taverner. "But I notice you talk to it as if it were real."

"By Jove, so I do!" said our visitor thoughtfully; "that is something new. I never used to do that. I took it for granted that the beast wasn't real, was only a phantom of my own brain, but recently a doubt has begun to creep in. Supposing the thing *is* real after all? Supposing it really has power to attack me? I have an underlying suspicion that my hound may not be altogether harmless after all."

"He will certainly be exceedingly dangerous to you if you lose your nerve and run away from him. So long as you keep your head, I do not think he will do you any harm."

"Precisely. But there is a point beyond which one may not keep one's head. Supposing, night after night, just as you were going off to sleep, you wake up knowing the creature is in the room, you see his snout coming round the corner of the curtain, and you pull yourself together and get rid of him and settle down again. Then just as you are getting drowsy, you take a last look round to make sure that all is safe, and you see something dark moving between you and the dying glow of the fire. You daren't go to sleep, and you can't keep awake. You may know perfectly well that it is all imagination, but that sort of thing wears you down if it is kept up night after night."

"You get it regularly every night?"

"Pretty nearly. Its habits are not absolutely regular, however, except that, now you come to mention it, it always gives me Friday night off; if it weren't for that, I should have gone under long ago. When Friday comes I say to it: 'Now, you brute, this is your beastly Sabbath,' and go to bed at eight and sleep the clock round."

"If you care to come down to my nursing home at Hindhead, we can probably keep the creature out of your room and ensure you a decent night's sleep," said Taverner. "But what we really want to know is—," he paused almost imperceptibly, "why your imagination should haunt you with dogs, and not, shall we say, with scarlet snakes in the time-honoured fashion."

"I wish it would," said our patient. "If it was snakes I could 'put more water with it' and drown them, but this slinking black beast—" He shrugged his shoulders and followed the butler out of the room.

"Well, Rhodes, what do you make of it?" asked my colleague after the door closed.

"On the face of it," I said, "it looks like an ordinary example of delusions, but I have seen enough of your queer cases not to limit myself to the internal mechanism of the mind alone. Do you consider it possible that we have another case of thought transference?"

"You are coming along," said Taverner, nodding his head at me approvingly. "When you first joined me, you would unhesitatingly have recommended bromide for all the ills the mind is heir to; now you recognize that there are more things in heaven and earth than were taught you in the medical schools.

"So you think we have a case of thought transference? I am inclined to think so too. When a patient tells you his delusions, he stands up for them, and often explains to you that they are psychic phenomena, but when a patient recounts psychic phenomena, he generally apologizes for them, and explains that they are delusions. But why doesn't the creature attack and be done with it, and why does it take its regular half-holiday as if it were under the Shop Hours Act?

"Friday, Friday," he ruminated. "What is there peculiar about Friday?"

He suddenly slapped his hand down on the desk.

"Friday is the day the Black Lodges meet. We must be on their trail again; they will get to know me before we have finished. Someone who got his occult training in a Black Lodge is responsible for that ghost hound. The reason that Martin gets to sleep in peace on Friday night is that his would-be murderer sits in Lodge that evening and cannot attend to his private affairs."

"His would-be murderer?" I questioned.

"Precisely. Anyone who sends a haunting like that to a man with a heart like Martin's knows that it means his death sooner or later. Supposing Martin got into a panic and took to his heels when he found the dog behind him in a lonely place?"

"He might last for half-a-mile," I said, "but I doubt if he would get any further."

"This is a clear case of mental assassination. Someone who is a trained occultist has created a thought-form of a black hound, and he is sufficiently in touch with Martin to be able to convey it to his mind by means of thought transference, and Martin sees, or thinks he sees, the image that the other man is visualizing.

"The actual thought form itself is harmless except for the fear it inspires, but should Martin lose his head and resort to vigorous physical means of defence, the effort would precipitate a heart attack, and he would drop dead without the slightest evidence to show who caused his death. One of these days we will raid those Black Lodges, Rhodes; they know too much. Ring up Martin at the Hotel Cecil and tell him we will drive him back with us tonight."

"How do you propose to handle the case?" I asked.

"The house is covered by a psychic bell jar, so the thing cannot get at him while he is under its protection. We will then find out who is the sender, and see if we can deal with him and stop it once and for all. It is no good disintegrating the creature, its master would only manufacture another; it is the man behind the dog that we must get at.

"We shall have to be careful, however, not to let Martin think we suspect he is in any danger, or he will lose his one defence against the creature, a belief in its unreality. That adds to our difficulties, because we daren't question him much, less we rouse his suspicions. We shall have to get at the facts of the case obliquely."

On the drive down to Hindhead, Taverner did a thing I had never heard him do before, talk to a patient about his occult theories. Sometimes, at the conclusion of a case, he would explain the laws underlying the phenomena in order to rid the unknown of its terrors and enable his patient to cope with them, but at the outset, never.

I listened in astonishment, and then I saw what Taverner was fishing for. He wanted to find out whether Martin had any knowledge of occultism himself, and used his own interest to waken the other's—if he had one.

My colleague's diplomacy bore instant fruit. Martin was also interested in these subjects, though his actual knowledge was nil—even I could see that.

"I wish you and Mortimer could meet," he said. "He is an awfully interesting chap. We used to sit up half the night talking of these things at one time."

"I should be delighted to meet your friend," said Taverner. "Do you think he could be persuaded to run down one Sunday and see us? I am always on the lookout for anyone I can learn something from."

"I—I am afraid I could not get hold of him now," said our companion, and lapsed into a preoccupied silence from which all Taverner's conversational efforts failed to rouse him. We had evidently struck some painful subject, and I saw my colleague make a mental note of the fact.

As soon as we got in, Taverner went straight to his study, opened the safe, and took out a card index file.

"Maffeo, Montague, Mortimer," he muttered, as he turned the cards over. "Anthony William Mortimer. Initiated into the

Order of the Cowled Brethren, October, 1912; took office as Armed Guard, May, 1915. Arrested on suspicion of espionage, March, 1916. Prosecuted for exerting undue influence in the making of his mother's will. (Everybody seems to go for him, and no one seems to be able to catch him.) Became Grand Master of the Lodge of Set the Destroyer. Knocks, two, three, two, password 'Jackal'.

"So much for Mr Mortimer. A good man to steer clear of, I should imagine. Now I wonder what Martin has done to upset him."

As we dared not question Martin, we observed him, and I very soon noticed that he watched the incoming posts with the greatest anxiety. He was always hanging about the hall when they arrived, and seized his scanty mail with eagerness, only to lapse immediately into despondency. Whatever letter it was that he was looking for never came. He did not express any surprise at this, however, and I concluded that he was rather hoping against hope than expecting something that might happen.

Then one day he could stand it no longer, and as for the twentieth time I unlocked the mailbag and informed him that there was nothing for him, he blurted out: "Do you believe that 'absence makes the heart grow fonder,' Dr Rhodes?"

"It depends on the nature," I said. "But I have usually observed if you have fallen out with someone, you are more ready to overlook his shortcomings when you have been away from him for a time."

"But if you are fond of someone?" he continued, half-anxiously, half-shamefacedly.

"It is my belief that love cools if it is not fed," I said. "The human mind has great powers of adaptation, and one gets used, sooner or later, to being without one's nearest and dearest."

"I think so, too," said Martin, and I saw him go off to seek consolation from his pipe in a lonely corner.

"So there is a woman in the case," said Taverner when I reported the incident. "I should rather like to have a look at her. I think I shall set up as a rival to Mortimer; if he sends black thought forms, let me see what I can do with a white one."

I guessed that Taverner meant to make use of the method of silent suggestion, of which he was a past-master.

Apparently Taverner's magic was not long in working, for a couple of days later I handed Martin a letter which caused his face to light up with pleasure, and sent him off to his room to read it in private. Half an hour later he came to me in the office and said:

"Dr Rhodes, would it be convenient if I had a couple of guests to lunch tomorrow?"

I assured him that this would be the case, and noted the change wrought in his appearance by the arrival of the long wished-for letter. He would have faced a pack of black dogs at that moment.

Next day I caught sight of Martin showing two ladies round the grounds, and when they came into the dining-room he introduced them as Mrs and Miss Hallam. There seemed to be something wrong with the girl, I thought; she was so curiously distrait and absent-minded. Martin, however, was in the seventh heaven; the man's transparent pleasure was almost amusing to witness. I was watching the little comedy with a covert smile, when suddenly it changed to tragedy.

As the girl stripped her gloves off she revealed a ring upon the third finger of her left hand. It was undoubtedly an engagement ring. I raised my eyes to Martin's face, and saw that his were fixed upon it. In the space of a few seconds the man crumpled; the happy little luncheon party was over. He strove to play his part as host, but the effort was pitiful to watch, and I was thankful when the close of the meal permitted me to withdraw.

I was not allowed to escape however. Taverner caught my arm as I was leaving the room and drew me out on to the terrace.

"Come along," he said. "I want to make friends with the Hallam family; they may be able to throw some light on our problem."

We found that Martin had paired off with the mother, so we had no difficulty in strolling round the garden with the girl between us. She seemed to welcome the arrangement, and we had not been together many minutes before the reason was made evident.

"Dr Taverner," she said, "may I talk to you about myself?"

"I shall be delighted, Miss Hallam," he replied. "What is it you want to ask me about?"

"I am so very puzzled about something. Is it possible to be in love with a person you don't like?"

"Quite possible," said Taverner, "but not likely to be very satisfactory."

"I am engaged to a man," she said, sliding her engagement ring on and off her finger, "whom I am madly, desperately in love with when he is not there, and as soon as he is present I feel a sense of horror and repulsion for him. When I am away, I long to be with him, and when I am with him, I feel as if everything were wrong and horrible. I cannot make myself clear, but do you grasp what I mean?"

"How did you come to get engaged to him?" asked Taverner.

"In the ordinary way. I have known him nearly as long as I have Billy," indicating Martin, who was just ahead of us, walking with the mother.

"No undue influence was used?" said Taverner.

"No, I don't think so. He just asked me to marry him, and I said I would."

"How long before that had you known that you would accept him if he proposed to you?"

"I don't know. I hadn't thought of it; in fact the engagement was as much a surprise to me as to everyone else. I had never thought of him in that way till about three weeks ago, and then I suddenly realized that he was the man I wanted to marry. It was a sudden impulse, but so strong and clear that I knew it was the thing for me to do."

"And you do not regret it?"

"I did not until today, but as I was sitting in the dining-room I suddenly felt how thankful I should be if I had not got to go back to Tony."

Taverner looked at me. "The psychic isolation of this house has its uses," he said. Then he turned to the girl again. "You don't suppose that it was Mr Mortimer's forceful personality that influenced your decision?"

I was secretly amused at Taverner's shot in the dark, and the way the girl walked blissfully into his trap.

"Oh, no," she said, "I often get those impulses; it was on just such a one that I came down here."

"Then," said Taverner, "it may well be on just such another that you got engaged to Mortimer, so I may as well tell you that it was I who was responsible for that impulse."

The girl stared at him in amazement.

"As soon as I knew of your existence I wanted to see you. There is a soul over there that is in my care at present, and I think you play a part in his welfare."

"I know I do," said the girl, gazing at the broad shoulders of the unconscious Martin with so much wistfulness and yearning that she clearly betrayed where her real feelings lay.

"Some people send telegrams when they wish to communicate, but I don't; I send thoughts, because I am certain they will be obeyed. A person may disregard a telegram, but he will act on a thought, because he believes it to be his own; though, of course, it is necessary that he should not suspect he is receiving suggestion, or he would probably turn round and do the exact opposite."

Miss Hallam stared at him in astonishment. "Is such a thing possible?" she exclaimed. "I can hardly believe it."

"You see that vase of scarlet geraniums to the left of the path? I will make your mother turn aside and pick one. Now watch."

We both gazed at the unconscious woman as Taverner concentrated his attention upon her, and sure enough, as they drew abreast of the vase, she turned aside and picked a scarlet blossom.

"What are you doing to our geraniums?" Taverner called to her.

"I am so sorry," she called back, "I am afraid I yielded to a sudden impulse."

"All thoughts are not generated within the mind that thinks

them," said Taverner. "We are constantly giving each other unconscious suggestion, and influencing minds without knowing it, and if a man who understands the power of thought deliberately trains his mind in its use, there are few things he cannot do."

We had regained the terrace in the course of our walk, and Taverner took his farewell and retired to the office. I followed him, and found him with the safe open and his card index upon the table.

"Well, Rhodes, what do you make of it all?" he greeted me.

"Martin and Mortimer after the same girl," said I. "And Mortimer uses for his private ends the same methods you use on your patients."

"Precisely," said Taverner. "An excellent object lesson in the ways of black and white occultism. We both study the human mind—we both study the hidden forces of nature; I use my knowledge for healing and Mortimer uses his for destruction."

"Taverner," I said, facing him, "what is to prevent you also from using your great knowledge for personal ends?"

"Several things, my friend," he replied. "In the first place, those who are taught as I am taught are (though I say it who shouldn't) picked men, carefully tested. Secondly, I am a member of an organization which would assuredly exact retribution for the abuse of its training; and, thirdly, knowing what I do, I dare not abuse the powers that have been entrusted to me. There is no such thing as a straight line in the universe; everything works in curves; therefore it is only a matter of time before that which you send out from your mind returns to it. Sooner or later Martin's dog will come home to its master."

Martin was absent from the evening meal, and Taverner immediately enquired his whereabouts.

"He walked over with his friends to the crossroads to put them on the 'bus for Hazlemere," someone volunteered, and Taverner, who did not seem too well satisfied, looked at his watch.

"It will be light for a couple of hours yet," he said. "If he is not in by dusk, Rhodes, let me know."

It was a grey evening, threatening storm, and darkness set in early. Soon after eight I sought Taverner in his study and said: "Martin isn't in yet, doctor."

"Then we had better go and look for him," said my colleague.

We went out by the window to avoid observation on the part of our other patients, and, making our way through the shrubberies, were soon out upon the moor.

"I wish we knew which way he would come," said Taverner. "There is a profusion of paths to choose from. We had better get on to high ground and watch for him with the field-glasses."

We made our way to a bluff topped with wind-torn Scotch firs, and Taverner swept the heather paths with his binoculars. A mile away he picked out a figure moving in our direction, but it was too far off for identification.

"Probably Martin," said my companion, "but we can't be sure yet. We had better stop up here and await events; if we drop down into the hollow we shall lose sight of him. You take the glasses; your eyes are better than mine. How infernally early it is getting dark tonight. We ought to have had another half-hour of daylight."

A cold wind had sprung up, making us shiver in our thin clothes, for we were both in evening dress and hatless. Heavy grey clouds were banking up in the west, and the trees moaned uneasily. The man out on the moor was moving at a good pace, looking neither to right nor left. Except for his solitary figure the grey waste was empty.

All of a sudden the swinging stride was interrupted; he looked over his shoulder, paused, and then quickened his pace. Then he looked over his shoulder again and broke into a half trot. After a few yards of this he dropped to a walk again, and held steadily on his way, refusing to turn his head.

I handed the glasses to Taverner.

"It's Martin right enough," he said; "and he has seen the dog."

We could make out now the path he was following, and, descending from the hill, set out at a rapid pace to meet him. We had gone about a quarter of a mile when a sound arose in the darkness ahead of us; the piercing, inarticulate shriek of a creature being hunted to death.

Taverner let out such a halloo as I did not think human lungs were capable of. We tore along the path to the crest of a rise, and as we raced down the opposite slope, we made out a figure struggling across the heather. Our white shirt fronts showed up plainly in the gathering dusk, and he headed towards us. It was Martin running for his life from the death hound.

I rapidly outdistanced Taverner, and caught the hunted man in my arms as we literally cannoned into each other in the narrow path. I could feel the played-out heart knocking like a badly-running engine against his side. I laid him flat on the ground, and Taverner coming up with his pocket medicine case, we did what we could.

We were only just in time. A few more yards and the man would have dropped. As I straightened my back and looked round into the darkness, I thanked God that I had not that horrible power of vision which would have enabled me to see what it was that had slunk off over the heather at our approach. That something went I had no doubt, for half a dozen sheep, grazing a few hundred yards away, scattered to give it passage.

We got Martin back to the house and sat up with him. It was touch-and-go with that ill-used heart, and we had to drug the racked nerves into oblivion.

Shortly after midnight Taverner went to the window and looked out.

"Come here, Rhodes," he said. "Do you see anything?"

I declared that I did not.

"It would be a very good thing for you if you did," declared Taverner. "You are much too fond of treating the thought-forms that a sick mind breeds as if, because they have no objective existence, they were innocuous. Now come along and see things from the view-point of the patient."

He commenced to beat a tattoo upon my forehead, using a peculiar syncopated rhythm. In a few moments I became conscious of a feeling as if a suppressed sneeze were working its way from my nose up into my skull. Then I noticed a faint luminosity appear in the darkness without, and I saw that a greyish-white film extended outside the window. Beyond that I saw the Death Hound!

A shadowy form gathered itself out of the darkness, took a run towards the window, and leapt up, only to drive its head against the grey film and fall back. Again it gathered itself together, and again it leapt, only to fall back baffled. A soundless baying seemed to come from the open jaws, and in the eyes gleamed a light that was not of this world. It was not the green luminosity of an animal, but a purplish grey reflected from some cold planet beyond the range of our senses.

"That is what Martin sees nightly," said Taverner, "only in his case the thing is actually in the room. Shall I open a way through the psychic bell jar it is hitting its nose against, and let it in?"

I shook my head and turned away from that nightmare vision. Taverner passed his hand rapidly across my forehead with a peculiar snatching movement.

"You are spared a good deal," he said, "but never forget that the delusions of a lunatic are just as real to him as that hound was to you."

We were working in the office next afternoon when I was summoned to interview a lady who was waiting in the hall. It was Miss Hallam, and I wondered what had brought her back so quickly.

"The butler tells me that Mr Martin is ill and I cannot see him, but I wonder if Dr Taverner could spare me a few minutes?"

I took her into the office, where my colleague expressed no surprise at her appearance.

"So you have sent back the ring?" he observed.

"Yes," she said. "How do you know? What magic are you working this time?"

"No magic, my dear Miss Hallman, only common sense. Something has frightened you. People are not often frightened to any great extent in ordinary civilized society, so I conclude that something extraordinary must have happened. I know you to be connected with a dangerous man, so I look in his direction. What are you likely to have done that could have roused his enmity? You have just been down here, away from his influence, and in the company of the man you used to care for; possibly you have undergone a revulsion of feeling. I want to find out, so I express my guess as a statement; you, thinking I know everything, make no attempt at denial, and therefore furnish me with the information I want."

"But, Dr Taverner," said the bewildered girl, "why do you trouble to do all this when I would have answered your question if you had asked me?"

"Because I want you to see for yourself the way in which it is possible to handle an unsuspecting person," said he. "Now tell me what brought you here."

"When I got back last night, I knew I could not marry Tony Mortimer," she said, "and in the morning I wrote to him and told him so. He came straight round to the house and asked to see me. I refused, for I knew that if I saw him I should be right back in his power again. He then sent up a message to say that he would not leave until he had spoken to me, and I got in a panic. I was afraid he would force his way upstairs, so I slipped out of the back door and took the train down here, for somehow I felt that you understood what was being done to me, and would be able to help. Of course, I know that he cannot put a pistol to my head and force me to marry him, but he has so much influence over me that I am afraid he may make me do it in spite of myself."

"I think," said Taverner, "that we shall have to deal drastically with Master Anthony Mortimer."

Taverner took her upstairs, and allowed her and Martin to look at each other for exactly one minute without speaking, and then handed her over to the care of the matron.

Towards the end of dinner that evening I was told that a gentleman desired to see the secretary, and went out to the hall to discover who our visitor might be. A tall, dark man with very peculiar eyes greeted me.

"I have called for Miss Hallam," he said.

"Miss Hallam?" I repeated as if mystified.

"Why, yes," he said, somewhat taken aback. "Isn't she here?"

"I will enquire of the matron," I answered.

I slipped back into the dining-room, and whispered to Taverner, "Mortimer is here."

He raised his eyebrows. "I will see him in the office," he said.

Thither we repaired, but before admitting our visitor, Taverner arranged the reading lamp on his desk in such a way that his own features were in deep shadow and practically invisible.

Then Mortimer was shown in. He assumed an authoritative manner. "I have come on behalf of her mother to fetch Miss Hallam home," said he. "I should be glad if you would inform her I am here."

"Miss Hallam will not be returning tonight, and has wired her mother to that effect."

"I did not ask you what Miss Hallam's plans were; I asked you to let her know I was here and wished to see her. I presume you are not going to offer any objection?"

"But I am," said Taverner. "I object strongly."

"Has Miss Hallam refused to see me?"

"I have not inquired."

"Then by what right do you take up this outrageous position?"

"By this right," said Taverner, and made a peculiar sign with his left hand. On the forefinger was a ring of most unusual workmanship that I had never seen before.

Mortimer jumped as if Taverner had put a pistol to his head; he leant across the desk and tried to distinguish the shadowed features, then his gaze fell upon the ring.

"The Senior of Seven," he gasped, and dropped back a pace. Then he turned and slunk towards the door, flinging over his shoulder such a glance of hate and fear as I had never seen before. I swear he bared his teeth and snarled.

"Brother Mortimer," said Taverner, "the dog returns to its kennel tonight."

"Let us go to one of the upstairs windows and see that he really takes himself off," went on Taverner.

From our vantage point we could see our late visitor making his way along the sandy road that led to Thursley. To my surprise, however, instead of keeping straight on, he turned and looked back.

"Is he going to return?" I said in surprise.

"I don't think so," said Taverner. "Now watch; something is going to happen."

Again Mortimer stopped and looked round, as if in surprise. Then he began to fight. Whatever it was that attacked him evidently leapt up, for he beat it away from his chest; then it circled round him, for he turned slowly so as to face it. Yard by yard he worked his way down the road, and was swallowed up in the gathering dusk.

"The hound is following its master home," said Taverner.

We heard next morning that the body of a strange man had been found near Bramshott. It was thought he had died of heart failure, for there were no marks of violence on his body.

"Six miles!" said Taverner. "He ran well!"